I0692947

# ¡SO vol 2

BY Vince
Suzukawa

Published by Sofawolf Press, Inc. • PO Box 11868 • Saint Paul, MN 55111-0868
http://www.sofawolf.com/

All characters, their distinctive likenesses and related indicia featured in this publication
are copyright © Vince Suzukawa. All stories copyright © Vince Suzukawa.
All artwork herein is copyright © Vince Suzukawa.

Book design and associated graphic elements are copyright © Sofawolf Press, Inc.

All rights reserved. No part of this publication may be reproduced by any means
without prior permission from the copyright owners.

Printed in the United States.

First trade paperback edition, June 2011 • POD Printing, June 2023
ISBN 978-1-936689-08-8

# Contents

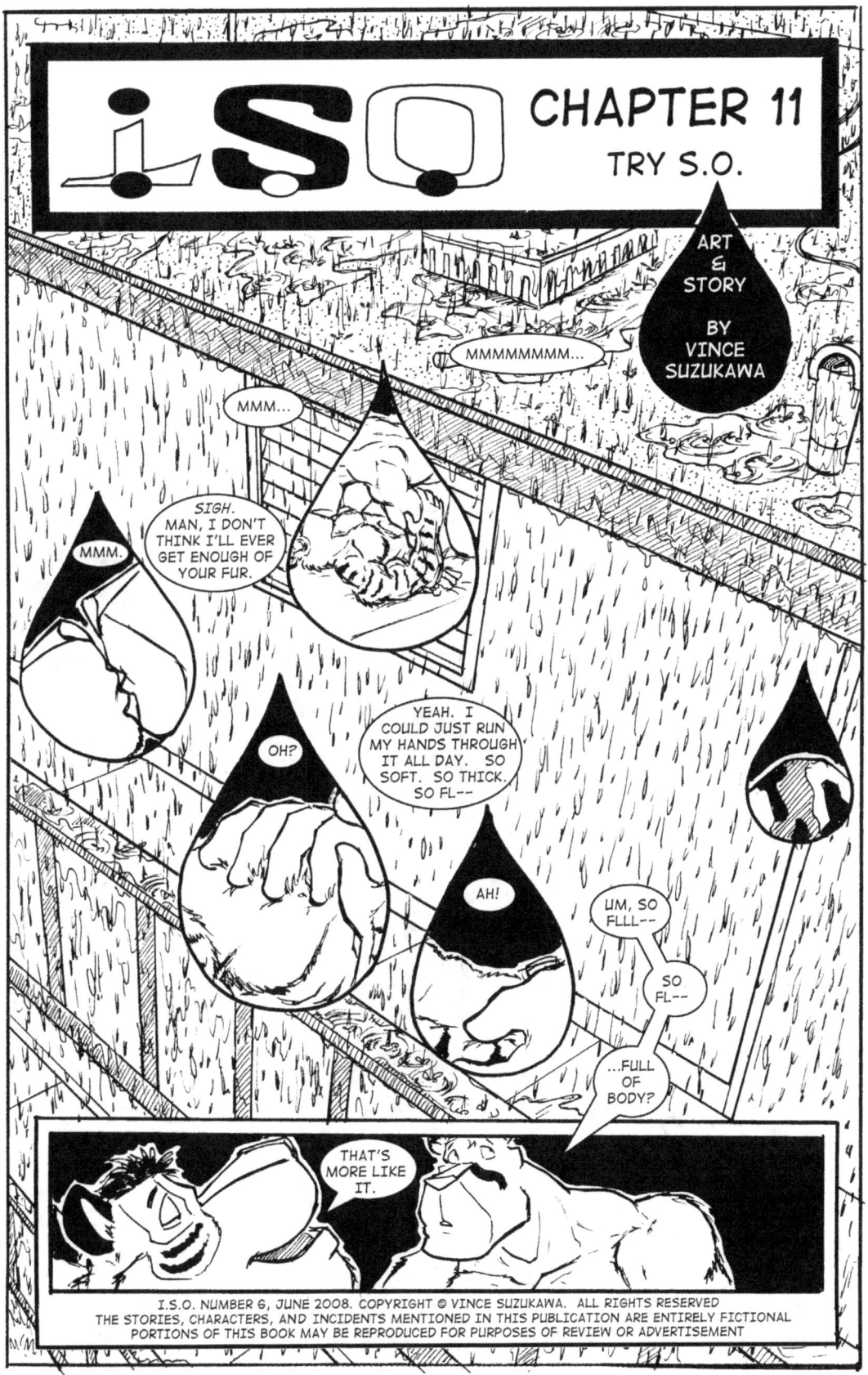

I.S.O. NUMBER 6, JUNE 2008. COPYRIGHT © VINCE SUZUKAWA. ALL RIGHTS RESERVED
THE STORIES, CHARACTERS, AND INCIDENTS MENTIONED IN THIS PUBLICATION ARE ENTIRELY FICTIONAL
PORTIONS OF THIS BOOK MAY BE REPRODUCED FOR PURPOSES OF REVIEW OR ADVERTISEMENT

OH, CODY. I UNDERSTAND WHY YOU KEEP LYING TO YOUR PARENTS, BUT...

SAM...AS YOUR GIRLFRIEND?!

ER...YUP. SO CAN YOU LIKE... BREAK THIS TO HER GENTLY?

THEN I'LL SEE HOW MUCH SHE'S WILLING TO GO ALONG WITH IT...

YOU REALIZE SHE'S GOING TO BE FURIOUS, RIGHT?

I'M EXPECTING THAT, YUP.

WELL, FOR STARTERS...

SHE'LL BE MORE FORGIVING IF YOU FESS UP YOURSELF. DON'T HAVE ME TALK TO HER FIRST.

CRAP. I WAS AFRAID OF THAT.

DOUG AND COVER!

CAN YOU AT LEAST COME WITH ME, SO THERE'LL BE A WITNESS TO THE MURDER?

DAMN.

I SHOULDN'T. I KNOW SHE'LL THINK YOU'RE USING ME TO GUILT HER INTO SAYING YES.

AND BEFORE SHE'LL AGREE, I BET SHE'LL MAKE ME--

PROBABLY...

GREAT, I'M DEAD. DO YOU MIND GRANTING A CONDEMNED MAN A SPECIAL LAST REQUEST?

SPECIAL REQUEST, HUH? WHAT'DYA HAVE IN MIND?

WAIT, NO, CONDEMNED MEN GET A LAST MEAL. SCREW THE RAIN, LET'S GO GET A STEAK.

NO, NO I'M SURE IT'S A LAST REQUEST...

3

4

7

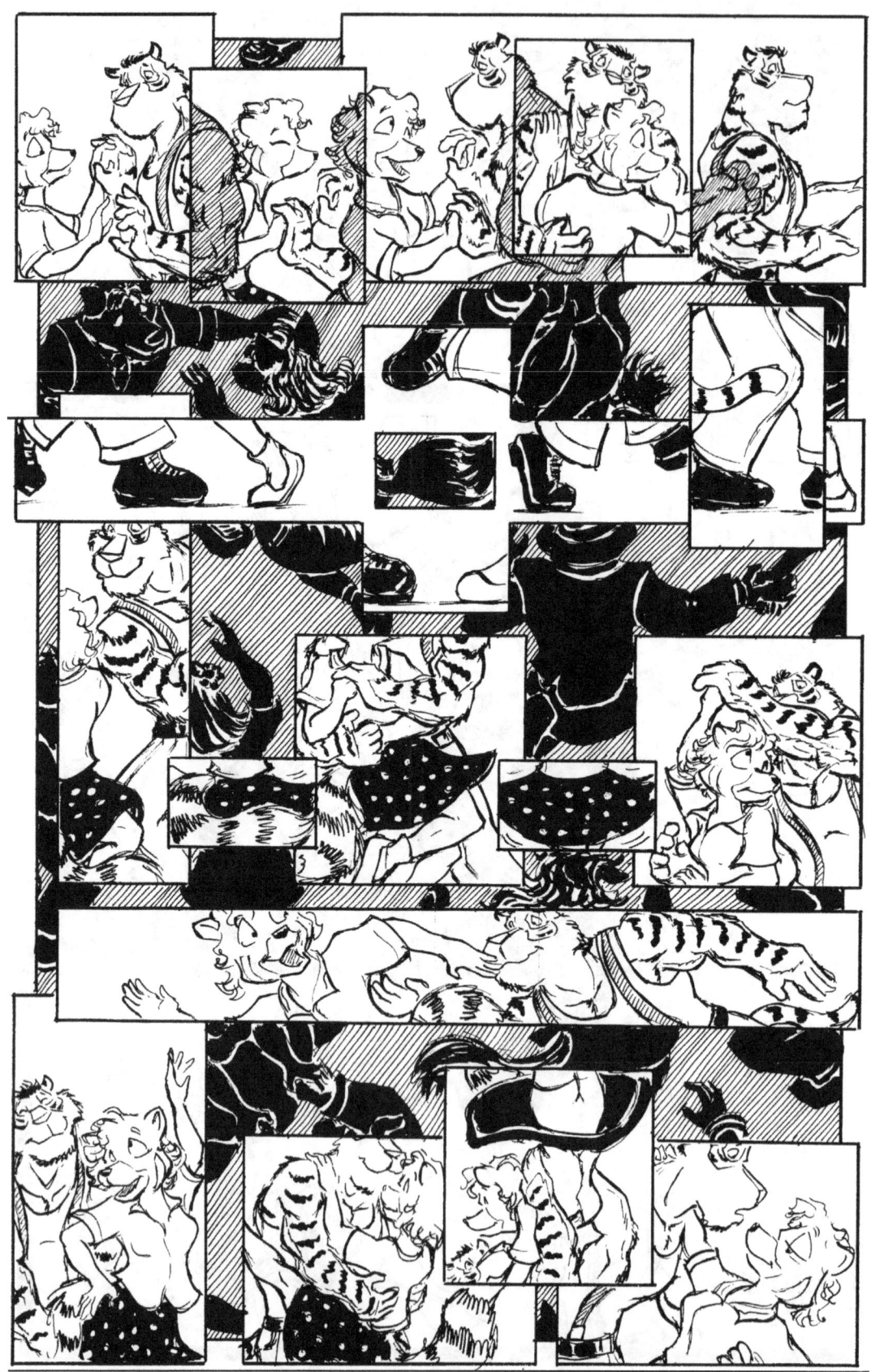

9

10

YOU CAN COME OUT NOW. GINO GOT RID OF HIM.

HE DID? PHEW.

YEAH, HE GETS REALLY SLEAZY WHEN HE'S HAD ONE TOO MANY. HE'S SUPPOSED TO GET BANNED IF THERE ARE ANY MORE COMPLAINTS BUT... I DON'T KNOW WHERE GINO IS NOW.

LEMME GUESS, WAS YOUR FRIEND ANYTHING LIKE ROY THERE?

ROY?

MAYBE I SHOULD DISPOSE OF HIM.

BUT...WAIT, I CAN'T.

SAM STILL THINKS I'M TOO AGGRESSIVE, SO EVEN IF THAT GUY'S BEING OBNOXIOUS, I CAN'T RISK LOOKING LIKE A PUNK. NOT WITH MEETING MY PARENTS AT STAKE...

WAIT HERE, NIKKI. I'LL BE RIGHT BACK...

ARE YOU GOING TO...? OH, BE CAREFUL!

OI! SO THAUT MUST BE JESSIE!

I WONDAH WHY CODY WOULD WANT T'KEEP 'ER A SECRET...

MAYBE—— AHEM!

OH. UH... 'ELLO AGAIN, MAITE.

11

12

13

14

OKAY, ALL YOU GUYS AND DOLLS...WE'RE GONNA SLOW IT DOWN SOME FOR THE LAST DANCE. YOU'VE BEEN A GREAT AUDIENCE! WE ARE THE BLACK AND WHITES. HIT IT!

WHOOPS. HEH, HOPE YOU WEREN'T SAVING THIS DANCE FOR SOMEONE ELSE. IF YOU'D RATHER NOT BOTHER WITH ME, I--

NO... S'OKAY.

SAY, CODY... THINK YOU'D BE UP FOR MORE LESSONS SOMETIME?

GOSH, NIKKI, I DUNNO...I'D HAVE TO ASK SAM IF IT'S OKAY IF I SEE OTHER PEOPLE, HEH-HEH!

SAM, IS IT OKAY IF HE SEES OTHER PEOPLE?

MM? 'COURSE.

SAM, IS EVERYTHING ALL RIGHT? YOU SEEM... PENSIVE.

OH. I'M FINE. REALLY.

HUH... ARE YOU LADIES GONNA BE OKAY FOR THE RIDE BACK? IT IS KINDA LATE. MAYBE I SHOULD COME WITH--

WELL, THAT'S VERY SWEET OF YOU, BUT IT'S ONLY A COUPLE STOPS, AND THERE'S ALL OF US HERE. BUT THANK YOU.

YOU GO ON HOME, STRIPEY.

DO NOT ENTER

TRAINS

CODY? UM, THANKS FOR... BEING A GOOD SPORT.

AW, MY END OF THE BARGAIN WAS EASY!

I--

BUT YOU, HAVING TO PRETEND TO LIKE ME? YA GOT SOME MAJOR PRACTICIN' AHEAD!

HEY, CODY! I'LL "SEE" YOU AROUND!

NOOO! RUN AWAY, RUN AWAY!

IT...MIGHT TAKE LESS THAN I THOUGHT...

15

SPEAKING OF WHICH, IF YOU'RE HAVING LUNCH WHERE YOU WORK, WON'T YOUR FOLKS EXPECT THE MEAL TO BE FREE?

EH, I'LL JUST PULL THE WAITRESS ASIDE TO PAY IT. I'LL SAY IT'S MOM'S BIRTHDAY OR SOMETHING.

OOH, NICE, A SON WHO TREATS HIS PARENTS TO A 24-HOUR DINER? PLUS THEY'LL ACCOST YOU WITH OFF-KEY SINGING AND A MINISCULE FREEBIE SUNDAE COVERED IN CANDLE WAX.

WELL, WHAT DO YOU WANT ME TO DO?

FOR STARTERS... ONE OF THE GUYS ON MY HOCKEY TEAM IS A MANAGER AT ROCKET JOHN'S.

THAT COUNTS AS A 24-HOUR DINER. MAYBE IF I TALK TO HIM, YOU COULD AT LEAST PRETEND TO WORK THERE CONVINCINGLY.

HEY, THANKS, I'D APPRECIATE THAT...

PERSONALLY, I STILL THINK YOU'RE ASKING FOR TROUBLE.

I MEAN, D'YOU KNOW HOW MANY SITCOM EPISODES HAVE BEEN BUILT AROUND A GUY PRETENDING TO DATE SOMEONE HE'S NOT? SOMETHING ALWAYS GOES WRONG!

BESIDES, THIS IS SAM WE'RE TALKING ABOUT HERE. I DOUBT SHE CAN BE TRUSTED TO PUT MUCH EFFORT INTO THIS.

YOU GUYS ARE BOTH RIGHT.

THAT'S EXACTLY WHY I'M HOPING THIS LUNCH IS A DISASTER.

HUH???

17

18

22

ANYWAY, SAM, MARTHA AND I WANTED TO THANK YOU.

THANK ME? FOR WHAT?

FOR THE DIFFERENCE YOU'VE MADE IN CODY!

SINGING IN THE RAI

AW, MA...

YOU DON'T SEE IT, CODY DEAR? NOW YOU'RE OUT AT CLUBS, YOU'VE GONE SWING DANCING, YOU'RE NOT WEARING A STITCH OF BLACK FOR ONCE, AND YOUR HAIRCUT ISN'T STRAIGHT OUT OF THE MARINES. YOU DON'T FEEL THAT YOU'VE BECOME A HAPPIER, MORE CAREFREE PERSON? REALLY, SAM, YA DONE GOOD.

UH...MY PLEASURE?

MAYBE WHAT HE NEEDED ALL THIS TIME WAS A WOMAN'S TOUCH.

OH...SOMEHOW, I DON'T THINK A WOMAN'S TOUCH WAS ER, QUITE THE SOLUTION.

SPARTACUS

WELL, YOU DID SOMETHING. HE WAS ALWAYS TRYING TO PLAY THE TOUGH GUY, AND IT WAS BEGINNING TO WORRY US.

"Rebel without a Cause"

THEN YOU CAUGHT HIS EYE. SAY, IF YOU DON'T MIND ME ASKING, SAM...I WAS JUST CURIOUS, HOW DID HE CATCH *YOURS?*

THE MONSTER THAT ATE MY BRAIN

HA! SHE'S TOTALLY GOING TO FREEZE UP HERE THINKING OF AN ANSWER.

OH, HE COMES ACROSS AS A BIT GRUFF AT FIRST, SURE. BUT HE WON ME OVER WITH A SENSITIVE SIDE I DON'T EVEN THINK *HE* KNEW HE HAD.

THE KING AND I

(IN) STEREO

YOU WON'T BELIEVE YOUR EARS!

YOU'LL LAUGH!

YOU'LL CRY!

SERIOUSLY, YOU SAW CODY'S SENSITIVE SIDE IN LESS THAN A YEAR, WITHOUT A SEARCH WARRANT?

A Streetcar Named Desire

COME NOW, YOU CAN BE HONEST. WAS IT A PHYSICAL THING? THAT'S HOW KARL AND I GOT PAST OUR FIRST BLIND DATE, AND LOOK AT US NOW! WHAT'S IMPORTANT IS THAT YOU TRULY CONNECTED AFTERWARDS, RIGHT?

SIN TH

...THAT'S WHEN WE LAUNCHED THE WHOLE "WHERE'S THE MEAT?" CAMPAIGN ON TV.

THOSE WERE A RIOT! MUST BE A FUN JOB.

AND WHAT DO YOUR PARENTS DO, SAM?

UM... THEY... UH...

HEY, I JUST REALIZED, DOU--YOU NEVER TOLD ME ANYTHING ABOUT THEM.

OH. YOU DON'T HAVE TO, IF IT'S PERSONAL.

NO, NO. I MEAN, I FIGURE WE'VE BEEN GOING OUT LONG ENOUGH.

I... HAVEN'T SPOKEN TO MY PARENTS IN ABOUT EIGHT YEARS, EVER SINCE THEY KICKED MY BROTHER OUT.

THEY'D HAD A BIG FIGHT, AND I WAS THE ONLY ONE WHO WOULD TAKE HIM IN.

WHAT?!

HE WAS ONLY FIFTEEN!

BUT THEY NEVER FORGAVE ME FOR THAT.

MY GOODNESS!

YOU WERE SO YOUNG. IT MUST'VE BEEN DIFFICULT SUPPORTING YOURSELF.

OH, IT WAS. IT TOOK A LOT LONGER TO FINISH MY DEGREE AT THE SAME TIME. BUT I MET...THE OWNER OF THIS PLACE AT MY SECOND JOB, AND HE INVITED ME ALONG HERE. HE PRETTY MUCH LETS ME RUN THE SHOW ON MY OWN, SO I'D SAY IT WORKED OUT FOR THE BEST.

AND REALLY, IF IT WASN'T FOR ALL THAT, I'D NEVER HAVE MET CODY HERE.

CODY!

GAH, WHY DID SHE GO THERE?

OH, HEY, THERE'S MARTY! WE, UH, NEED TO DISCUSS HIS... SCHEDULE FOR NEXT WEEK, SWEETIE.

OF COURSE! WE'LL BE RIGHT BACK!

24

ON A MORE SERIOUS TOPIC...

WHAT YOU SAID ABOUT YOUR PARENTS AND DOUG...THEY KICKED HIM OUT CUZ HE CAME OUT?

SIGH. NO, EVEN WORSE...

THEY CAUGHT HIM IN THE ACT, WITH A SENIOR WHO HAD PERSUADED HIM TO RISK IT.

I'M SURPRISED THEY EVEN TOOK THE TIME TO SCREAM AT HIM BEFORE THEY THREW HIM OUT.

NOW YOU KNOW WHY I AGREED TO HELP YOU OUT RIGHT AWAY. I WOULDN'T WISH AN INVOLUNTARY OUTING ON MY WORST ENEMY.

AND THAT'S WHAT MAKES YOU SO PARANOID ABOUT WHO HE DATES, RIGHT?

UM... ACTUALLY, IT'S A LOT MORE COMPLICATED THAN THAT.

OH?

DOUG HAS... LET'S JUST SAY, AN UNHEALTHY INTEREST IN BAD BOYS.

HE FALLS FOR GUYS WHO PUSH HIM AROUND, BECAUSE HE *WANTS* THEM TO.

SOME TAKE ADVANTAGE OF HIM MORE THAN OTHERS; BUT ONCE, ONE DESPERATELY NEEDED TO "BORROW" MONEY. MORE THAN DOUG COULD AFFORD. BUT HE FELL FOR IT, AND THEN OF COURSE, NEVER HEARD FROM HIM AGAIN.

THAT PIECE OF--! IS THAT WHY DOUG IS WORKING HIS ASS OFF AT TWO JOBS?

YUP.

NEEDLESS TO SAY, I KNEW RIGHT OFF THE BAT HE'D BE HOPING YOU WERE INTERESTED. AND WHEN YOU WERE, I WAS AFRAID IT'D--

--END IN DISASTER, LIKE ALWAYS.

CODY, YOU PIG!

YEAH. BUT...THANKS FOR PROVING ME WRONG.

ANYTIME.

*I JUST DON'T KNOW WHY YOU HAD TO BE THE ONE TO TELL ME...*

30

YOU USED ME!

AND NOT EVEN IN A GOOD WAY!

YOU LIED TO ME!

WELL, I--

YOU MADE YOUR GOOFY ROOMMATE MANHANDLE ME!

HOW COULD YOU DO THIS TO ME? OH! I'M SO TRAUMATIZED! I'LL NEVER TRUST ANY MAN AGAIN!

AND THE AWARD FOR ACTRESS MOST LIKELY TO GO DIRECT-TO-VIDEO GOES TO... BECKY ADAMS!

AW, SHE AD-LIBBED PRETTY WELL TOO.

WELL, WHEN SAM POINTED OUT YOUR PARENTS, I KNEW I COULDN'T SAY YOU'D NEVER DATE ME CUZ WE SIMPLY DON'T SEE EYE TO..."EYES."

BUT REALLY, SORRY FOR DRAGGING YOU INTO THAT, BECKY. AND THANKS.

HM...YOU COULD SHOW YOUR GRATITUDE BY DOING OUR CLEANUP DUTIES FOR THE REST OF THE WEEK, PERHAPS.

EH, IT'S COOL.

D'OH. SAM, DID YOU TELL EVERYONE?

OH MAN, TYRONE WAS ROLLING ON THE CEILING!

AWW, I WAS THINKING WE'D HAVE SOME MAKE-UP SEX INSTEAD, BABYDOLL.

A NICE WIDDLE MENAGE-A-TROIS?

GYAAH, NO! NO FAIR! OKAY, OKAY, THE REST OF THE WEEK IT IS!

THE REST OF THE YEAR? AGH! WAIT, NO, NOT THE RIBS!!!

SO... ANY LAST REQUESTS?

DON'T JUST STAND THERE, HELP MEHEE!

JAKE? WHERE ARE YOU?

CODY--

I'M SORRY FOR ALL THE TROUBLE I CAUSED. I GUESS YOU WERE RIGHT TO ALWAYS TRY AVOIDING ME. BUT NO WORRIES. I WON'T BOTHER YOU ANY LONGER. THE SEMESTER'S OVER SOON, AND I'LL STAY OUT OF YOUR WAY UNTIL THEN. TAKE CARE, AND HAVE A GOOD HOLIDAY.

JAKE.

OH, NO.

DAMMIT, JAKE. IT WASN'T YOUR FAULT. WHY'D YOU RUN OFF WITHOUT TALKING TO ME FIRST? YOU MUST KNOW BY NOW I'M NOT OUT TO KICK YOUR ASS...RIGHT?

I HAVE TO EXPLAIN TO HIM WHAT HAPPENED. UH...CRAP. I NEVER GOT HIS PHONE NUMBER. HELL, I DON'T EVEN KNOW HIS CLASS SCHEDULE. I NEVER...ASKED.

WELL, YOU HAD WANTED TO GET HIM OFF YOUR BACK ALL THIS TIME, CODY. I HOPE YOU'RE HAPPY WITH YOURSELF.

I.S.O. NUMBER 7, JANUARY 2009, COPYRIGHT © VINCE SUZUKAWA. ALL RIGHTS RESERVED
THE STORIES, CHARACTERS, AND INCIDENTS MENTIONED IN THIS PUBLICATION ARE ENTIRELY FICTIONAL
PORTIONS OF THIS BOOK MAY BE REPRODUCED FOR PURPOSES OF REVIEW OR ADVERTISEMENT

34

WHOA WHOA WHOA!

OKAY, NOW LIKE, STEADY... STEADY...

SEE, I DON'T GET IT, MY BALANCE THIS PAST TERM IS SHOT.

MAN, IS HE CUTE.

BUT THE EXCELLENT NEWS IS I THINK I'VE TOTALLY FIGURED OUT WHY.

REALLY?

OH!

GOTCHA!

WELL... LIKE, HOW TO PUT IT.

WERE YOU A...UH...LATE BLOOMER?

UM. MAYBE. WHAT MAKES YOU SAY THAT?

S'JUST THAT JAKE SHOWED ME YOUR FAMILY PHOTO...

IT LOOKED PRETTY RECENT, BUT YER FIGURE SEEMED, UH... DIFFERENT.

I MEAN, UH, DON'T GET ME WRONG! YOU WERE STILL HOT, JUST LESS...Y'KNOW... BODACIOUS.

SO IF YOU, LIKE, KINDA GOT EXTRA TOPHEAVY QUICKLY, IT'D SO THROW OFF YER BALANCE.

ONE GIRL ON THE SQUAD TWO YEARS AGO WAS LIKE THAT. BUMMER.

HUH. NO KIDDING.

DID HE JUST CALL ME HOT?

YEAH! BUT SHE GOT USED TO IT, AND I'M SURE YOU WILL TOO.

OOH, THANKS, ZACH! YOU'RE A GENIUS!

NEVAH THOUGHT AI'D HEAH THAUT PHRAISE.

ANYTIME, DUDETTE!

KIDS? OH, THERE YOU ARE!

35

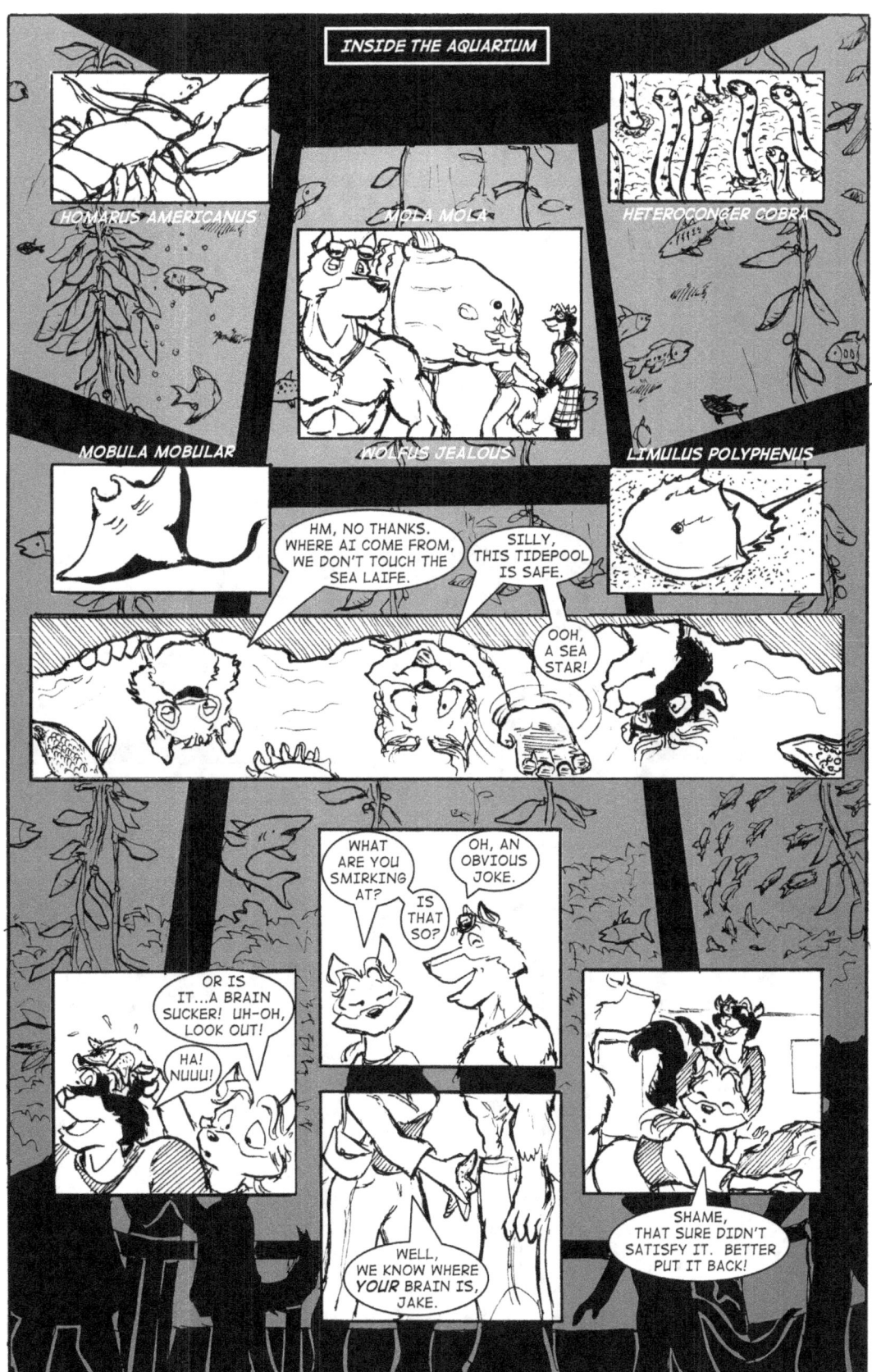

40

41

42

**Panel 1:**

SO DOES IT, LIKE, BUG YOU THAT HE SLEEPS AROUND?

DON'T *YOU* THINK IT'S DISGUSTING?

ERM, WELL, HE SEZ HE PLAYS IT SAFE. AND IT'S NOT LIKE, Y'KNOW, HE HAS'TA FORCE HIMSELF ON 'EM. IT TAKES TWO TO HORIZONTAL TANGO.

**Panel 2:**

BUT I'M SURE EVERYONE CAN TELL HE'S A PLAYER...YET SOMEHOW, PEOPLE STILL FALL FOR HIS SO-CALLED "CHARM."

I SHOULDN'T GO THERE...BUT, EH, HE DIDN'T NOTICE ME FLIRTING BEFORE.

NOT A TRAP. HONEST!

**Panel 3:**

I MEAN, WHO WANTS TO DRINK FROM THE SAME FOUNTAIN EVERYONE ELSE USES, SO TO SPEAK?

I DUNNO, I GUESS SOME PEOPLE FIND CONFIDENCE HOT. ME, I WAY PREFER IT WHEN--OOH, WHADOIDONOW, WHADOIDO-NOW?

SHOOT THE OVERHANG! NO, THE UPPER ONE! THERE!

KEWL, THANKS! SO, LIKE, UM...YOU'RE SAYIN' YOU WANNA SLEEP AROUND TOO?

WHA? OH, NO NO NO! AHEH, IT JUST SEEMS UNFAIR THAT JAKE GETS TO HAVE HIS CAKE, AND EAT IT TOO.

**Panel 4:**

WHEREAS IF *I* WANT TO CATCH SOME REALLY CUTE GUY'S ATTENTION, I CAN'T GET AWAY WITH ONE-TENTH OF THE FLIRTING JAKE DOES WITHOUT BEING CALLED ON IT.

IT WOULD BE NICE IF I DIDN'T HAVE TO SECOND-GUESS MYSELF.

IF IT HELPS... SOME GUYS DON'T EVEN TRY TO FIGURE OUT THE SIGNALS ANYONE SENDS, CUZ THEY GET CONFUSED WAY EASILY, AND IT'S MADE THEIR BRAINS IMPLODE BEFORE.

IT'S WHEN THEY'RE *NOT* FLIRTING THAT'S IMPORTANT. IF THEY'RE LIKE... HELPFUL. AND FUN. AND FUNNY. AND, Y'KNOW, WILL TALK TO HIM LIKE HE'S, LIKE, A REAL PERSON.

**Panel 5:**

THINK THAT'D WORK ON Y--ER, SOME GUYS?

OH YEAH. TOTALLY.

44

SO...HE DIDN'T SAY ANYTHING ABOUT ME THEN, HUH?

EH, FLIRTING'S ALL PAURT OF THE GAIME.

'FRAID NOT. AND YOU SAW ME FLIRTING WITH HIM, WHY DIDN'T YOU STOP ME?

HM, AI REALLY CAUN'T CRITICAIZE.

...JUST NEVAH THOUGHT AI'D LOSE. AND REALLY, AI DIDN'T THINK YOU TWO WOULD MOVE SO FAST. YOU'VE ONLY KNOWN 'IM--

UH...

GUESS AI'VE BEEN A PRETTY POAH EXAMPLE...

HE'S SWEET AND HELPFUL, AND NOT AFRAID TO SHOW A BIT OF VULNERABILITY.

I LIKE A GUY WHO'S AWARE OF HIS SHORTCOMINGS BUT STILL WILLING TO SHOW OFF.

DOES THIS MEAN YOU'RE... ACTUALLY INTERESTED IN HIM, TOO? MOAH THAN JUST AS A ONE NAIGHT FLING?

I CAN'T SAY I'M POSITIVE IT'D WORK IN THE LONG TERM, BUT I AT LEAST WOULD GIVE IT A SHOT, SINCE HE'LL BE HERE FOR SCHOOL FOR A FEW YEARS.

OF COURSE, I WAS GOING BY MORE THAN JUST HORMONES.

HE'S HONEST AND STRAIGHT-FORWARD... I DON'T THINK HE KNOWS HOW TO BE MANIPULATIVE.

BUT THAT'S ALL STUFF YOU KNEW ABOUT...S'WHY YOU WERE AFTER HIM TOO?

UH. OF COAHSE.

WE HAVE ATHLETICS AND CHEERLEADING IN COMMON.

HEH. AND CUZ HE'S GOT A REALLY NICE ASS, I KNOW.

YOU'D BETTER NOT BE THINKING HE ISN'T SMART ENOUGH FOR ME?

EH, MAI SAIDE OF THE FAMILY WOS NEVAH INTO ROCKET SCIENCE...

I GUESS IF IT DIDN'T BOTHAH YOUR MUM, IT WON'T BOTHAH YOU.

AI'M JUST WONDERIN' WOT ZACH THINKS OF ALL THIS.

LET'S ASK HIM.

UM...DUDE, LIKE, WE NEED TO TALK...

45

47

48

WELL, YOU ARE A JOCK... SURELY YOUV'E ENCOUNTERED OTHER HOT, FRIENDLY GUYS BESIDES TODD.

'COURSE. AND DON'T CALL ME SHIRLEY!

AND, FOR A LONG TIME, I BET YOU WERE THE BIGGEST GUY IN YOUR SCHOOL... MAYBE EVEN YOUR DIVISIONS. EVERYONE KNEW IT...CUZ YOU'D MAKE SURE THEY KNEW IT.

I'VE SEEN YOU AMP UP THE TESTOSTERONE WHENEVER YOU'RE AROUND OTHER BIG GUYS... LIKE WITH THOR. YOU GO ALL...ALPHA MALE. DOMINANT. AND I'D GUESS YOU WIN ANY PISSING MATCH YOU START.

SO YOU KEPT ALL HUNKY GUYS AT ARM'S DISTANCE, BY FORCE. CUZ BASICALLY, THE FURTHER THEY WERE, THE LESS LIKELY YOU'D GET TEMPTED. OR NOTICED.

BUT DOUG WAS A DIFFERENT STORY. FOR THE FIRST TIME, THERE WAS SOMEONE THAT YOU COULDN'T FORCE TO BACK AWAY. YOU HAD NO IDEA WHAT ELSE TO DO... AND YOUR ONLY CHOICE WAS TO GIVE IN TO YOUR HORMONES.

THEN, DOUG TURNED OUT TO BE SUBMISSIVE. YET NOW YOU ASSOCIATE BEING DOMINANT WITH EMOTIONAL DISTANCE, NOT INTIMACY. SO THAT'S GOT THE TWO OF YOU AT A STALEMATE. YOU JUST NEED TO FIGURE OUT HOW TO GET AROUND THAT.

WAIT WAIT, HOLD ON A SEC, JEFF...

Downloading...

LET'S GET ON WITH THIS.

CREAK

!!!

BRUNO TANAKIN © D. NOTO

NOVENTA © C. ZAWADZKI

58

59

YOU KNOW MY DATE WITH SAM THAT YOU WALKED IN ON? IT WAS ALL A FAKE, A BIG SHOW FOR MY PARENTS. WE WERE PLANNING TO BREAK UP THEN ANYWAY.

THERE'S NO BECKY OR JESSIE OR WHATEVER. SO YOU DIDN'T RUIN ANYTHING...IN FACT, YOU HELPED MIX THINGS UP A BIT JUST AS WE KINDA GOT STUCK.

REALLY? BUT...WHY FAKE IT?

I DIDN'T WANT TO TELL THEM... I'M GAY.

I WAS HOPING YOU'D LOOK A BIT MORE SHOCKED.

ERM, NO, AI THINK AI GET IT.

AI MEAN, SAM ALWAYS DID STRAIKE ME AS A BIT OF A BALLBUSTAH...AI CAN SEE 'ER TURNING A GUY OFF WOMEN PERMANENTLY.

OR...DO YOU MEAN YOU STARTED QUESTIONING YOURSELF CUZ THAUT FAINE SPECIMEN OF A WOMAN DID NOTHIN' TO HOIST YER MAINSAIL?

WHAT? NO NO NO, I DIDN'T FIGURE IT OUT JUST NOW; I'VE KNOWN FOR SIX YEARS. SAM AGREED TO PRETEND TO BE MY GIRLFRIEND FOR THAT NIGHT.

IT WASN'T THAT. YOU WERE JUST SO...FORWARD. I THOUGHT...YOU'D, KINDA POUNCE ME THE INSTANT YOU FOUND OUT WE BOTH LIKE MEN.

SIGH. YEAH, 'FRAID SO.

YOU MEAN... FROM THE FIRST TAIME WE MET, YOU DIDN'T WANT ME TO KNOW YOU WERE GAY? AW, CODY...YOU SHOULDA KNOWN AI'D BE THE LAUST BLOKE TO JUDGE YOU ABOUT IT.

OI. AI CAME ACROSS AS THAUT MUCH OF A SEXUAL PREDATAH?

AHEM

EH, AI SUPPOSE AI DESERVE THAUT. BUT CROSS MAI HEART...EVERY ENCOUNTAH AI'VE 'AD HAS BEEN 100% CONSENSUAL. IF YOU WERE UNWILLING, AI'D NEVAH 'AVE TOUCHED YOU.

WHO SAYS I WOULD'VE BEEN UNWILLING?

60

WOT?!

THAT'S RIGHT. IF YOU'D STARTED ANYTHING, I WAS WORRIED I WOULDN'T STOP YOU.

SERIOUSLY?

SERIOUSLY. JAKE, YOU WERE THE HOTTEST GUY I'D EVER MET IN MY LIFE.

EVERYTHING YOU DO IS A MASSIVE TURN-ON. THE WAY YOU MOVE, THE WAY YOU...SORTA DRESS, THE WAY YOU CRINKLE YOUR EYES WHEN YOU SMILE. *EVERYTHING.*

IT WAS A CONSTANT BARRAGE OF TEMPTATION BEING IN THE SAME ROOM WITH YOU.

WHEN I FIRST SAW YOU ON THE AIRPLANE, IT TOOK EVERY OUNCE OF SELF-RESTRAINT I HAD TO NOT TACKLE YOU TO THE GROUND THEN AND THERE AND RUN MY TONGUE UP AND DOWN THOSE PERFECT WASHBOARD ABS OF YOURS.

OI! AI'M VERY FLATTERED, MAITE, THANKS. BUT WOULD IT 'AVE BEEN SUCH A CRAIME IF YOU HAD GIVEN INTO YOUR HORMONES? YOU WEREN'T SEEING ANYONE, WERE YOU?

NO, BUT I AM NOW. AND I DUNNO, I'M FREAKING OUT ABOUT LETTING GO WITH HIM, TOO.

WELL, THAUT'S PRESSURE TO PERFORM. WITH ME, AI JUST WOULD'VE WANTED TO 'AVE FUN, NO STRINGS ATTACHED. YOU COULD'VE EXPERIMENTED. MAYBE YOU'RE JUST OVAHTHINKING IT.

HE'S GOT A POINT, THOUGH. DOUG WASN'T YOUR ONLY OPTION--AT LEAST, NOT AT FIRST. SO... THERE'S JAKE, WHO'S FORWARD AND WILLING, AND THEN DOUG WAY AT THE OTHER END OF THE SPECTRUM, WHO'S QUIET AND SUBMISSIVE. AND YOU'RE EQUALLY SHY WITH BOTH OF THEM? SO IF THIS ISN'T JUST ABOUT DOUG, THEN WHAT IS IT? STOP THINKING OF THE BAGGAGE WITH DOUG. OR JAKE. OR JEFF, OR TODD, OR NATE, OR ANYONE YOU'VE HAD SEXUAL TENSION WITH... WHAT'S REALLY PUTTING THE KIBOSH ON YOUR LIBIDO?

MAYBE I WANTED MORE THAN JUST A FLING.

OR MAYBE...

BEEP
BEEP
BOOP

CLICK

...IT'S CUZ IT WOULD'VE MEANT I WAS GAY.

ERM, DIDN'T WE JUST GO THROUGH THIS? YOU SAID YOU WERE--?

HEH, OKAY, I KNOW THAT MAY NOT MAKE MUCH SENSE, BUT...IT'S JUST...WELL, I'M STILL, ERM...A VIRGIN. AND HAVING SEX, TO ME, WAS KINDA THE POINT OF NO RETURN HERE.

SEE, I KNEW I WAS INTERESTED IN THE MALE BODY FOR YEARS. I LIKED HOW IT LOOKED, HOW IT FELT... YES, EVEN THE WAY IT SMELLED...

AND I HAD ZERO INTEREST IN THE FEMALE BODY, SO THE SIMPLEST CONCLUSION WAS THAT I WAS GAY.

BUT THERE WAS ALWAYS THE REASSURANCE THAT MAYBE, JUST MAYBE, MY FASCINATION IN THE MALE BODY AMOUNTED TO NOTHING MORE THAN ADMIRATION FOR SOMETHING WELL-CONSTRUCTED.

LIKE...THE WAY ALMOST ANYONE WILL CONSIDER A FERRARI NICER TO EXPERIENCE THAN A PINTO. MAYBE I WAS ACTUALLY ASEXUAL.

UNTIL I HAD... WELL, SEXUAL RELATIONS WITH A GUY...

AND... *LIKED* IT...

THEN *TECHNICALLY* I WASN'T HOMOSEXUAL, RIGHT?

AT LEAST THAT WAS BETTER THAN BEING A FLAMING QUEER, RIGHT? MAYBE I COULD APPEAR TO HAVE A NORMAL LIFE AS THE "PERPETUAL BACHELOR." SURE, THAT STILL MAKES SOME PEOPLE WONDER, BUT NOTHING LIKE WHEN YOU HAVE A MALE "ROOMMATE" YOUR WHOLE LIFE.

SO THAT'S IT. EVERYTHING ELSE HAS BEEN EXCUSES AND SPECULATION AND THEORIES AND DEFINITIONS. BUT I KNEW ONCE I GAVE INTO MY SEXUAL URGES--REALLY, WHETHER IT WAS WITH A GUY OR NOT--THAT WOULD BE IT, DEFINITIVELY. AND I WASN'T PREPARED FOR THAT.

I GUESS THIS MAKES IT THE FINAL TEST.

AND I CAN'T KEEP RUNNING FROM IT. I HAVE TO KNOW FOR SURE.

62

63

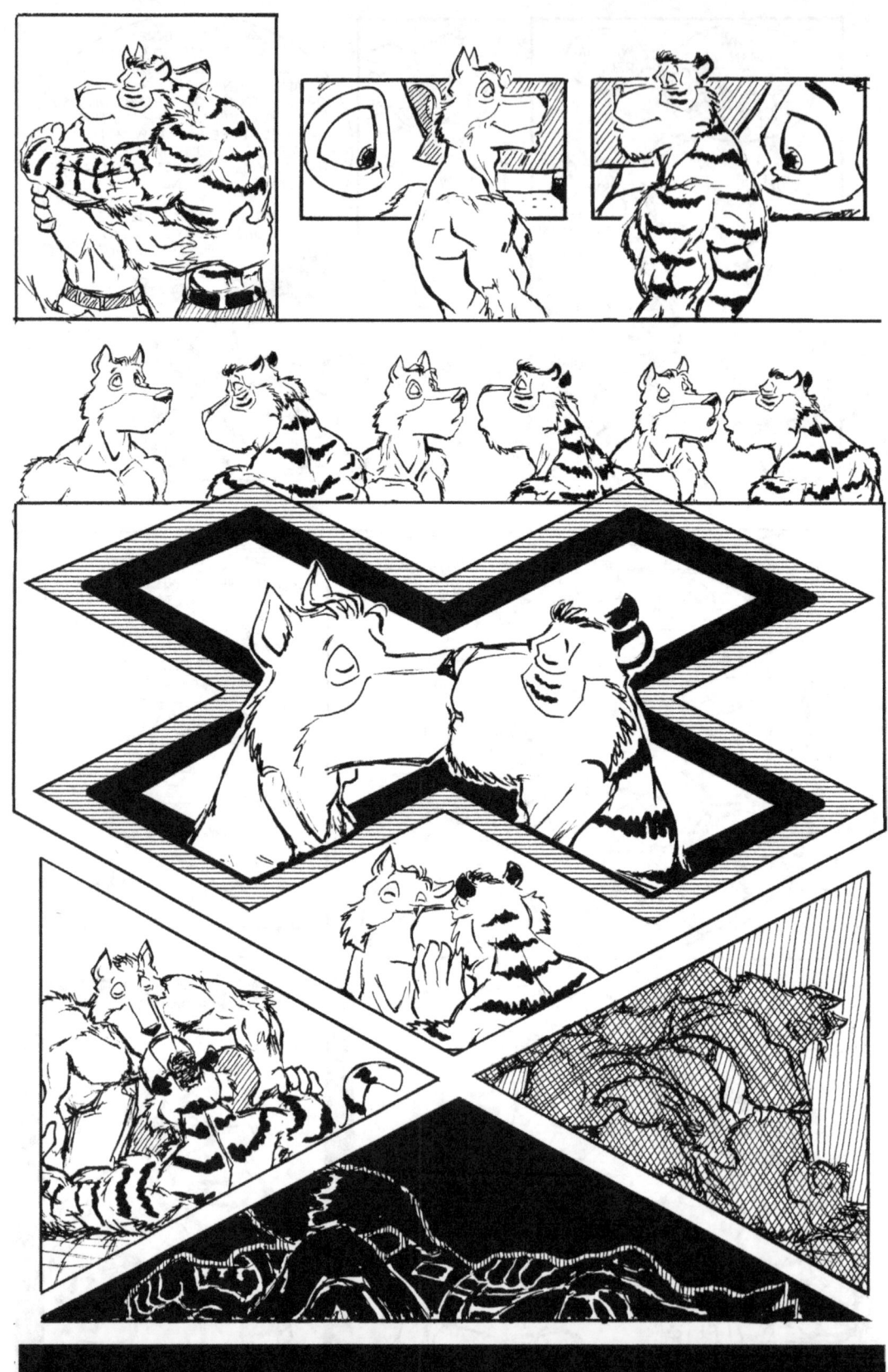

# CHAPTER 15
## EYES OPEN

ART & STORY BY VINCE SUZUKAWA

I.S.O. NUMBER 8, JULY 2009 COPYRIGHT © VINCE SUZUKAWA. ALL RIGHTS RESERVED
THE STORIES, CHARACTERS, AND INCIDENTS MENTIONED IN THIS PUBLICATION ARE ENTIRELY FICTIONAL
PORTIONS OF THIS BOOK MAY BE REPRODUCED FOR PURPOSES OF REVIEW OR ADVERTISEMENT

STILL...I DO HAVE A BOYFRIEND, AS I SAID. I REALLY SHOULDN'T HAVE DONE ANY OF THAT.

AW, WE DIDN'T GO VERY FAR, MAITE. IT'S ALL TOTALLY FOHGIVEABLE, IF YOU ASK ME.

SURE, WE PLAYED TONSIL TENNIS FOAH A BIT, BUT YOU STOPPED ME. LOOKED A BIT GUILTY, DON'CHA REMEMBAH?

HONESTLY, I DON'T.

WELL, T'BE HONEST...AI SURE WANTED TO KEEP GOIN', BUT LAIKE AI SAID...IT ALWAYS HAS TO BE CONSENSUAL.

OKAY, AI COULDN'T RESIST SNUGGLIN' YOU A BIT AFTAHWAHDS...NO STRINGS ATTACHED, MAIND YOU. BUT AI THINK YOU WERE ALREADY ASLEEP BAI THEN.

AND THEN THE BUNK FELT A BIT SMALL, SO I CAME UP HEAH. JEFF 'AS NOTHIN' TO WORREH ABOUT.

HECK, IF IT MAIKES 'IM FEEL BETTAH, YOU MUTTERED 'IS NAIME IN YOUR SLEEP--

WAIT... "JEFF"?!

67

68

69

BREAK UP? WHERE DID THAT COME FROM? I CAN'T JUST DO THAT.

CAN I?

ISN'T DOUG EVERYTHING YOU WANTED IN A BOYFRIEND? OR AT LEAST...WHAT YOU THOUGHT YOU WANTED?

SURE. HE'S NICE, SWEET, EASYGOING, AND INCREDIBLY HOT...WELL, JUST LIKE JEFF. AND JAKE. AND HECK, EVEN NATE, AND TODD. WHAT MAKES YOUR RELATIONSHIP WITH DOUG UNIQUE?

HE'S...QUIET. PASSIVE. WHICH SHOULD'VE BEEN THE PERFECT MATCH FOR THE BIG OL' MACHO TIGER. HE'S PRETTY MUCH WHAT EVERYONE EXPECTED YOU TO END UP WITH. PARTICULARLY DOUG HIMSELF. AND YOU'RE NOT LIVING UP TO THAT.

YOU THOUGHT YOU COULD. BUT SO MUCH HAS HAPPENED OVER THE PAST FEW MONTHS.

MAYBE IT IS BETTER TO STEP BACK. MAYBE YOU NEED TO ASK DOUG IF HE'S SEEN THE REAL YOU. AND YOU NEED TO SHOW HIM. TELL HIM. BECAUSE YOU JUST FEEL AWKWARD WHEN HE HAS ANY EXPECTATIONS.

AND IT SHOULDN'T BE AWKWARD; IT SHOULD BE NATURAL. YOU FEEL HAPPY WHEN YOU JUST HANG OUT WITH HIM...AS YOU SHOULD. BUT MAYBE THAT JUST MAKES YOU FRIENDS. AND DOUG DESERVES MORE THAN THAT.

SO. WOW.

NOW THAT YOU'VE LAID ALL THE CARDS ON THE TABLE...YOU SURE YOU CAN'T TAKE THINGS ANY FURTHER FROM HERE?

UM...YOU SEEM RATHER SURPRISED.

YEAH, SORTA. YOU MEAN YOU'RE NOT?

I WAS... KIND OF BRACING MYSELF FOR THIS ALL WEEKEND. AND I'VE BEEN THINKING ABOUT THIS FOR AWHILE.

AWHILE, HUH? BUT YOU JUST DROP IT LIKE THAT ON ME, WITH NO WARNING?

NO, NO, I WAS PLANNING TO GIVE YOU ONE LAST CHANCE ON OUR DATE TONIGHT...

REALISTICALLY, THOUGH? I WAS ALMOST POSITIVE NOTHING WAS GOING TO HAPPEN.

SO I'D DECIDED, IF YOU BAILED AGAIN, THEN--

WELL, ONLY IF YOU INSIST ON PUTTING IT THAT WAY, CUZ--

WHAT, IS THAT WHAT THIS ENTIRE RELATIONSHIP IS BUILT AROUND? COME ON, IT'S JUST SEX!

IF IT'S "JUST SEX", THEN *WHY THE HELL WOULDN'T YOU DO IT WITH ME?*

THEN WHAT? YOU WERE GOING TO DUMP ME... OVER SEX?

TOUCHE'...

72

I APPRECIATE THAT YOU NEEDED SOME TIME. BUT WE'RE MEN. AND I KNOW ALL MEN INEVITABLY GET...

...URGES. AND OFTEN TIMES, THEY CAN'T RESIST ACTING ON THEM.

EVEN YOU?

YES, BUT NOT IF I COULD HELP IT. AND IT WAS DIFFICULT. REALLY DIFFICULT. HECK... I SORTA HAVE A CRUSH ON TIM, AND HE'D BE AN EASY OUTLET...BUT WE NEVER FOLLOWED THROUGH WITH IT.

WE RESPECT THE BOUNDARIES OF RELATIONSHIPS; IT'S EITHER ALL OR NOTHING. DITTO FOR ROBBIE AND TREVOR...AND THEY'VE ALL SUPPORTED ME ON THIS.

BUT I KNOW I'M AN UNUSUAL CASE, AND IT'S GETTING HARDER TO FIND YOUNG GAY GUYS WHO FEEL THE SAME WAY.

THE ODDS OF SOMEONE BEING UNFAITHFUL ARE BAD ENOUGH. AND WHEN THEY REFUSE TO DO ANYTHING WITH YOU EITHER...IT RAISES SUSPICIONS. AND PEOPLE WILL TALK...

WHAT, SO YOU ALL EXPECTED ME TO CHEAT ON YOU?

NOT NECESSARILY. BUT YOU CAN ONLY HOLD OUT FOR SO LONG... THERE HAS TO BE *SOME* RELEASE. YOU ALMOST GAVE IN ONCE, AND YOU DON'T SEEM ALL THAT... ATTUNED TO YOUR HORMONES.

YEAH, WELL, I...

SO YOU DID--!

WAIT, WAIT, LET ME EXPLAIN!

I FINALLY STRAIGHTENED THINGS OUT IN MY HEAD OVER THE WEEKEND.

IT'S NOT THAT I WAS AFRAID OF SEX PER SE, I WAS JUST STALLING ON CONFIRMING MY ORIENTATION. SEX WITH A MAN WOULD BE... SEALING THE DEAL, BASICALLY.

BUT OF COURSE, I WAS GOING TO HAVE TO MAKE THAT LEAP EVENTUALLY, AND ACCEPTING THAT NOW KINDA LIFTED THE MENTAL BLOCK.

THE THING IS, AS SOON AS I SORTED ALL THIS OUT, I...

...IMMEDIATELY MADE OUT WITH MY HOT AND VERY PROMISCUOUS ROOMMATE...

...AND FOLLOWED *THAT* UP WITH A MASSIVELY EROTIC DREAM ABOUT THE FRIEND WHO I'D JUST PUSHED AWAY CUZ I FEARED I WAS FALLING FOR HIM!

...REALIZED YOU WEREN'T THE FIRST GUY I WANTED TO SHARE THAT WITH.

THIS WAS NO SPONTANEOUS URGE. NO OUTBURST OR LOSS OF CONTROL. THIS WAS JUST FINALLY ALLOWING MYSELF TO EXPERIENCE WHAT FELT RIGHT, FOR THE FIRST TIME.

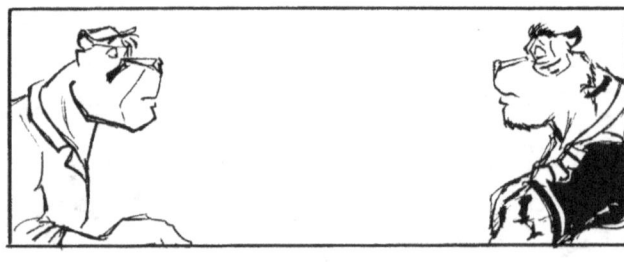

I SEE.

SORRY.

75

I DUNNO, I JUST HAD THIS VISION OF YOU AS A BOUNCER.

HEY, I'VE SEEN YOU IN ACTION. YOU'D EASILY DISPOSE OF ANY PROBLEMS BEFORE THEY GET OUT OF HAND.

ME? I DON'T EVEN OWN ANY BLACK CLOTHING!

I'LL HAVE TO PRACTICE MY SCOWLING FIRST...

PHEW, DEFLECTED THAT ISSUE. NOW I JUST GOTTA JAM--

BESIDES, YOU ALREADY ARE THE--

OH. I GET IT.

YOU'RE QUITTING THE HANGOUT, CUZ... *SIGH* I THOUGHT MAYBE YOU'D TALKED DOUG OUT OF BREAKING UP, BUT...UM, YEAH. BUMMER.

I DON'T KNOW IF I HAVE MUCH CHOICE. IT WAS A MUTUAL DECISION FOR DOUG AND ME BUT...IT COULD GET AWKWARD WITH SAM THERE. I'LL BET SHE'S GONNA BE *PISSED*.

SAM'S A TOUGH COOKIE, FOR SURE. BUT SHE ONLY WANTS THE BEST FOR DOUG.

AND I THINK NOW SHE'S AWARE THAT YOU DO TOO.

THANKS, TIM.

TAKE CARE...

IF IT HELPS, CODY...YOU'RE NEW TO DATING. AND THE ODDS OF FINDING YOUR LIFE PARTNER ON THE VERY FIRST TRY... ARE PRETTY SLIM. SAM KNEW THE ODDS. AND...I THINK EVEN DOUG DID, TOO.

ALL IN ALL, THAT WAS SURPRISINGLY DRAMA-FREE. NO WATER WORKS, SHOUTING, BROKEN DISHES...

I THOUGHT IT WOULD HURT MORE TO...HURT TO...TO...

T-TODD? CALL ME WHEN YOU LAND? PLEASE? THANKS... *CHOKE*

78

SO LEMME GET THIS STRAIGHT, BRO. YOU DON'T EVEN KNOW WHAT HE HAS TO SAY, AND YOU'RE ALREADY FREAKIN' OUT OVER IT?

WELL, THEY'RE RIGHT, THIS REALLY ISN'T A GOOD TIME.

CODY, IS THERE *EVER* A GOOD TIME WITH YOU?

LOOKY HERE, MAN. WHENEVER SOMETHING DOES NOT GO EXACTLY ACCORDING TO PLAN-- AS LIFE OFTEN DOES--YOU TURN TAIL! YOU EITHER HOPE THINGS WORK OUT FOR THE BEST, OR YOU WAIT UNTIL SOMEONE CHASES YOU DOWN AND CORNERS YOU.

ONCE IN A WHILE, YOU NEED TO GROW UP, GROW A PAIR, AND MEET THINGS HEAD ON!

WELL, I...

HUH. Y'KNOW... HE'S SEEN OR HEARD ABOUT IT ALL THE TIME...WHENEVER SOMEONE CONFRONTS ME, I...

BRRING-BRRING

BENEFRIENDS?

BED FRIENDS?

EJECT! EJECT!

BEST FRIENDS?

BOYFRIENDS?

ALL I'M SAYIN', IS OPEN COMMUNICATION IS THE BEST WAY TO SORT OUT YOUR PROBLEMS. TAKE IT FROM SOMEONE WHO KNOWS.

Y'KNOW, HE'S RIGHT.

TOTALLY. GO ON, PICK IT UP. WE'RE RIGHT HERE IF YOU NEED US.

BRRRING-BRRRING

BRRRING-BRRRING

HEY, JEFF? SORRY 'BOUT THAT...

81

HEY. THANKS FOR COMING OUT HERE.

NO PROB. YOU GOIN' ALL NATURE BOY ON ME?

IN THIS CAR? HA! I ONLY WANTED SOME PRIVACY. BUT...IT'S GOOD TO SEE YOU. I HATED JUST LEAVING THINGS THE WAY THEY WERE.

YEAH, LIKEWISE...

I'M... SORRY TO HEAR ABOUT DOUG.

THANKS. HE AND I KINDA AGREED IT WASN'T MEANT TO BE.

STILL... THAT'S WHY I CALLED IN THE FIRST PLACE...

I'D WANTED TO APOLOGIZE FOR OVERSTEPPING MY BOUNDARIES AS A FRIEND. WE WOULDN'T HAVE FOUGHT IF I'D JUST DROPPED IT.

AW, YOU DON'T HAVE TO DO THAT. YOU KNEW I WANTED YOUR HELP.

HELP, SURE, BUT NOT INTERFERENCE. YOU WERE ALREADY OVERTHINKING, YOU DIDN'T NEED PSYCHOBABBLE ON TOP OF THAT...BUT I KEPT PICKING YOUR BRAIN APART ANYWAY. I SHOULD HAVE LET YOU FIGURE THINGS OUT ON YOUR OWN.

CODY...I WAS...PUSHING YOU TO STAY WITH DOUG, EVEN THOUGH I KINDA DOUBTED YOU'D LAST.

HUH? W-WHY WOULD YOU DO THAT?

BECAUSE I WANTED YOU.

OKAY, JUST CUZ YOU ADMITTED THAT ALREADY, DOESN'T MEAN IT MAKES ANY MORE SENSE...

I KNOW, I KNOW, I'LL EXPLAIN...

WHEN WE FIRST MET, I COULD TELL YOU NEEDED A FRIEND. WHEN IT TURNED OUT YOU NEEDED A MENTOR, I FELT IT WAS MORE IMPORTANT TO BE THERE FOR YOU IN THAT CAPACITY, THAN WORRY IF I WAS GOING TO FALL FOR YOU.

AND THEN WE HAD A LOT OF FUN TOGETHER, AND... YEAH, I FELL FOR YOU. MUCH EARLIER THAN I'VE LET ON, REALLY. IT WAS STUPID OF ME, BUT I DID. STILL, YOU WERE SO DISTRACTED WITH DOUG, I HOPED YOU WOULDN'T NOTICE.

SO I DID ALL I COULD TO HELP THINGS ALONG...AND MORE BEYOND THAT. DOUG SEEMED LIKE A SWEET, QUALITY GUY, AND I WAS HAPPY WHEN YOU TWO FINALLY HOOKED UP.

I HONESTLY WASN'T SURE HOW COMPATIBLE YOU GUYS WOULD BE TOGETHER, BUT I FIGURED ONCE YOU WERE SET UP WITH HIM, YOU COULD HANDLE IT FROM THERE.

INSTEAD, YOU KEPT COMING TO ME FOR ADVICE...AND PART OF ME WONDERED IF YOU WANTED MORE. AND WHILE I WAS HAPPY TO COUNSEL YOU, IT JUST MADE US EVEN CLOSER.

AND ALL THE WHILE, I KNEW I WAS BEING OBSERVED. AND I KNEW THAT NO MATTER HOW I TRIED TO HIDE MY FEELINGS, IT WAS DANGEROUS FOR US TO BE AS CLOSE AS WE WERE.

SO THE MORE ASSISTANCE I COULD GIVE TO KEEP YOUR RELATIONSHIP WITH DOUG GOING, THE BETTER. MAYBE IF I GRABBED AT ENOUGH STRAWS, THERE'D BE A BREAKTHROUGH THAT'D STICK. CUZ THAT WAS THE ONLY WAY I COULD AVOID AROUSING ANY MORE SUSPICION. THE ONLY WAY I COULD PROTECT YOU.

THAT'S CRAZY. WHAT KINDA CONSPIRACY IS THIS? "PROTECT" ME? PROTECT ME FROM WHO?

MY SISTER, MAUREEN.

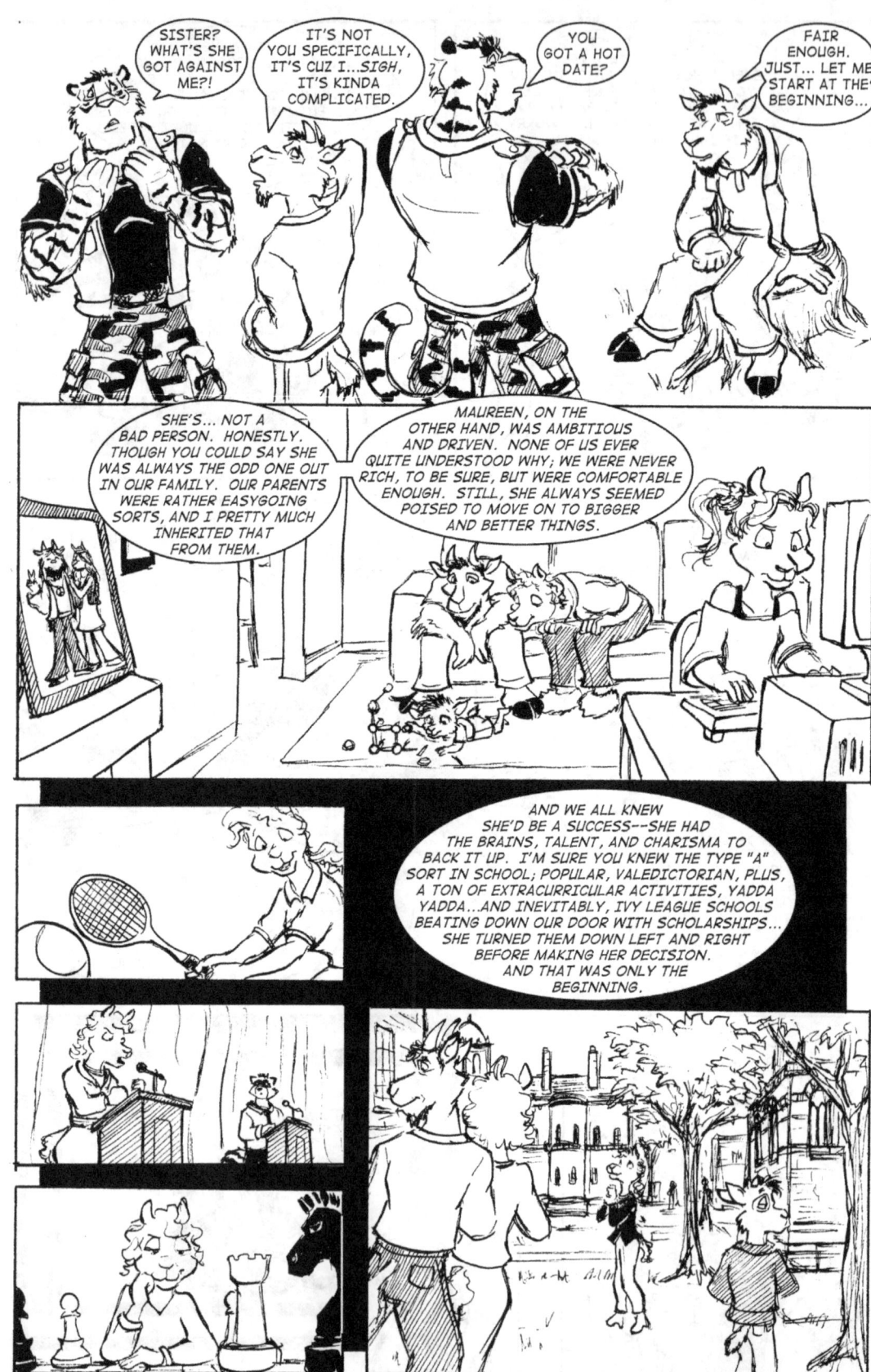

REALLY, THOUGH, I THINK SHE FRETTED TOO MUCH ABOUT FITTING IN. HER WORK ALWAYS SPOKE FOR ITSELF.

IT TURNED OUT TO BE A BIT OF A CULTURE SHOCK BEING AROUND SOME OF THE WEALTHIER STUDENTS. MORE THAN EVER, I THINK SHE WANTED TO BE A PART OF THAT WORLD.

AND SPEAK IT DID. SHE GRADUATED MAGNA CUM LAUDE, MADE SHORT WORK OF THE LSAT, AND WENT STRAIGHT TO LAW SCHOOL. WE WERE WORRIED SHE'D BURN HERSELF OUT, BUT SHE RATHER SEEMED TO ENJOY THE CHALLENGE.

BUT MY PARENTS NEVER GOT TO SEE HER GET HER LAW DEGREE. THEY WERE BOTH KILLED IN A CAR ACCIDENT JUST BEFORE SHE GRADUATED.

WHAT? OH, MAN, JEFF. I'M SO SORRY. I HAD NO IDEA...YOU NEVER TALK ABOUT THEM.

THANKS, BUT...WELL, THERE WAS OTHER BAGGAGE I DIDN'T WANT TO BRING UP.

Y'SEE, THE OTHER DRIVER GOT OFF PRETTY EASILY. I WASN'T PLEASED BY THIS, BUT I BELIEVE ACCIDENTS HAPPEN.

MAUREEN, ON THE OTHER HAND, WAS REALLY BITTER ABOUT IT, BLAMING THE JUDGE FOR THE SENTENCE. THAT KIND OF SOLIDIFIED HER DECISION TO BECOME A JUDGE HERSELF--AND AS SOON AS SHE COULD.

SHE'D ALWAYS BEEN THE ONE WITH A STRONG SENSE OF JUSTICE, I GUESS.

ONCE SHE'D SECURED HER FIRST JOB, HER MISSION WAS CLEAR. IT'D TAKE A LOT OF WORK TO ACCELERATE THE GAME PLAN AS MUCH AS SHE INTENDED, BUT SHE WAS GOING TO DO IT.

THERE WAS ONLY ONE SACRIFICE THAT WOULD HAVE TO BE MADE. BUT SHE FELT SHE'D BE ABLE TO GET TO IT AT SOME POINT.

87

SO OVER THE COURSE OF THAT YEAR, I PICKED UP VARIOUS TIDBITS ABOUT WENDELL.

HE WAS AN ONLY CHILD, FRESH OFF AN EXTENSIVE EDUCATION, AND HIS DOTING FAMILY DIDN'T KNOW WHAT ELSE TO DO WITH HIM EVER SINCE HE DECIDED HE WAS GOING TO WRITE THE NEXT GREAT AMERICAN NOVEL...THEY KINDA LEFT HIM TO HIS OWN DEVICES ALONE IN THIS BIG HOUSE.

AND I GOT TO THINKING...

MAUREEN'S BIOLOGICAL CLOCK WAS TICKING LOUDER AS SHE APPROACHED THIRTY, AND I KNOW SHE WAS RECEPTIVE TO MEETING MR. RIGHT, BUT HER JOB LEFT NO TIME TO SEARCH.

THEN HERE'S WENDELL; THE SENSITIVE NEW-AGE SORT, VERY BRIGHT, WELL-MANNERED, EXCELLENT LINEAGE...AND MOST IMPORTANTLY, WRITING A BOOK AFFORDED HIM THE FLEXBILE SCHEDULE FOR DATING A WORKAHOLIC LAWYER.

PLUS I KNEW MAUREEN PREFERRED A STAY-AT-HOME HUSBAND OVER A NANNY-- NO DOUBT SHE COULD AFFORD IT. STILL, THAT REALLY NARROWED HER OPTIONS.

BUT I FINALLY MANAGED TO COAX OUT OF WENDELL THAT HE DID, INDEED, TRULY WANT TO HAVE KIDS--AND NOT SOLELY BECAUSE HIS FAMILY WAS PRESSURING HIM FOR GRANDCHILDREN.

THAT WAS ALL I NEEDED TO HEAR TO INTRODUCE THE TWO OF THEM.

I ONLY HOPED THEY'D HIT IT OFF.

88

IN FACT, THEY TURNED OUT TO BE AN EXCELLENT MATCH. HE WAS NOT INTIMIDATED BY HER INTELLIGENCE AND CAREER. SHE LEARNED A LITTLE MORE ABOUT SPONTANEITY FROM HIM.

HE GAVE HER THE INROADS TO HIGH SOCIETY SHE HAD DREAMED OF IN COLLEGE. AND AS HE WAS A FEW YEARS YOUNGER AND A LITTLE SHELTERED, HE DIDN'T MIND LETTING HER BE THE WORLDLY ONE.

HOWEVER, SHE CONSTANTLY WORRIED SHE WAS TOO "LOW CLASS"--IF NOT FOR HIM, FOR HIS ENTIRE FAMILY SHE RAVED ABOUT WHAT A PROPER GENTLEMAN HE WAS, HOW TRADITIONAL HIS VALUES WERE...IT WAS ONLY LATER THAT I FIGURED OUT WHAT SHE MEANT. IT MADE ANY ADVANCEMENT IN THEIR RELATIONSHIP DOWNRIGHT GLACIAL, BUT SHE DIDN'T WANT TO OFFEND HIM, OR HIS FAMILY.

SHE SHOULDN'T HAVE WORRIED ABOUT HIS FAMILY; THEY THOUGHT HIGHLY OF HER, AND NO DOUBT THE PROSPECT OF HAVING A FUTURE JUSTICE AROUND DIDN'T HURT. I, ON THE OTHER HAND, WAS JUST A GRUNGY LITTLE REPAIRMAN, NOT TO MENTION BY NOW I HAD A STEADY BOYFRIEND... I SERIOUSLY DOUBTED HIS CONSERVATIVE FAMILY WOULD THINK MUCH OF ME. SO I LAID LOW, AND KEPT TO MYSELF. BUT I DIDN'T MIND...I HAD MY OWN LIFE, AND THERE WAS NO POINT IN RUINING HER CHANCE AT HAPPINESS.

A COUPLE MORE YEARS PASSED, AND WENDELL KEPT STALLING ON POPPING THE BIG QUESTION--IN SPITE OF MANY HINTS. MAUREEN WAS GETTING IMPATIENT, BUT SHE KNEW HOW TRADITIONAL HE WAS, AND WANTED TO LET HIM DO THINGS HIS WAY. SURELY IT WOULD ONLY BE A MATTER OF TIME.

THANKFULLY, IT WAS.

EVERYTHING WENT SMOOTHLY UNTIL THE BACHELOR PARTY, WHERE TWO OF WENDELL'S BUDDIES RECRUITED ME TO PLAY A LITTLE JOKE ON HIM.

HE WAS SUCH A PROPER LITTLE GUY, HE'D NEVER SEEN A STRIPPER, AND THEY'D HIRED SOME BABE TO GIVE HIM A LAPDANCE. BUT FIRST, THEY WANTED TO THROW HIM OFF BY HAVING ME POP OUT BEFORE THEY BROUGHT HER OUT.

I REALLY DIDN'T WANT TO, BUT I WAS THE ONLY ONE THERE WITH THE BODY FOR IT, AND SOON I WAS TOO DRUNK TO CARE.

SO I PLAYED ALONG, HE PLAYED ALONG, AND EVERYONE HAD A GOOD LAUGH.

UNTIL, WELL...

THEY FOUND OUT WE WEREN'T JUST PLAYING ALONG.

SO...YEAH. WENDELL MADE A FULL CONFESSION...AND APOLOGY. HE WAS GAY, ALWAYS HAD BEEN.

AND WHILE HE REALLY DID WANT KIDS OF HIS OWN, HE WASN'T USING MAUREEN JUST FOR THAT; HE WAS QUITE FOND OF HER, AND HAD HOPED HE COULD TELL HER THE TRUTH...

AT SOME POINT.

PERHAPS IF SHE TRULY LOVED HIM BACK, THEY COULD HAVE WORKED SOMETHING OUT. MAYBE EVEN INDEFINITELY, FOR THE SAKE OF THE CHILDREN.

BUT I'D THROWN A HUGE WRENCH IN THAT PLAN. I FELT TERRIBLE.

AW, YOU WERE DRUNK. HELL, HE WAS TOO! AND IT WASN'T EVEN YOUR IDEA.

IT WASN'T THAT... JUST THAT I'D KEPT MY ORIENTATION SECRET. IF I'D TOLD MAUREEN OR WENDELL EARLIER, THE END RESULT MIGHT HAVE HAVE BEEN THE SAME--MAYBE WENDELL WOULD'VE FOUND THE COURAGE TO COME OUT TO AN ALLY--BUT AT LEAST IT WOULDN'T HAVE EXPLODED SO PUBLICLY. WITH ALL THE GOSSIP FLYING AROUND, MAUREEN WAS FURIOUS AT ME.

THAT'S NOBODY'S BUSINESS BUT YOURS! YOU WEREN'T RESPONSIBLE FOR WENDELL'S COVER-UP!

WELL, WHOEVER'S FAULT IT WAS...THE WEDDING WAS OBVIOUSLY CALLED OFF AFTER THAT.

MAUREEN NEVER HEARD FROM WENDELL AGAIN; THE FAMILY BLAMED HER FOR BRINGING THE SO-CALLED "CORRUPTING INFLUENCE"--ME--TO THE SITUATION.

FORTUNATELY, IT'S GONE NO FURTHER THAN THAT... THEY HAVEN'T TRIED TO SABOTAGE HER CAREER OR ANYTHING. PROBABLY BECAUSE SHE SAID...ER, SCREAMED?...SHE WAS CUTTING ALL TIES WITH ME AFTERWARDS.

I TRIED TO CONTACT HER ONCE THINGS HAD COOLED DOWN A LITTLE, BUT SHE NEVER RETURNED MY CALLS.

HI, YOU'VE REACHED 555-3773. PLEASE LEAVE A MESSAGE--

EVENTUALLY, I FELT I HAD TO JUST MOVE ON WITH MY LIFE.

WHICH I NEVER COULD'VE DONE WITHOUT THE SUPPORT OF MY BOYFRIEND JEREMY.

92

I'LL NEVER FORGET HOW COMPOSED SHE WAS...

YOU HAD NO RIGHT TO DO THAT! YOUR BEEF IS WITH ME; JEREMY'S DONE NOTHING WRONG!

DONE NOTHING WRONG? WHY WAS HE SKULKING AROUND, HIDING THINGS, LYING TO HIS PARENTS?

YOU KNOW DAMN WELL WHY, AND IT'S NONE OF YOUR BUSINESS, ANYWAY!

ISN'T IT? TELL ME, BROTHER DEAR, HOW IS CAITLIN?

CAITLIN? WHAT'S SHE GOT TO DO WITH--

I SAW HIS WEBJOURNAL. JEREMY KNEW HE WAS GAY WHILE THEY WERE DATING, OR AT LEAST PRETENDING TO, RIGHT?

WELL--

I... I DON'T KNOW.

WAS SHE HIS BEARD FOR HIS PARENTS? DID HE BREAK HER HEART?

DON'T KNOW, OR DON'T CARE?

I--

AND WEREN'T *YOU* BANGING...WHAT'S HER NAME, LESLIE, IN HIGH SCHOOL?

AW, DON'T LOOK AT ME LIKE THAT. *SOME* OF US EXPERIMENTED MORE THAN YOU!

SORRY, SORRY, GO ON...

YEAH, BUT...

· · ·

YOU THINK I *ENJOYED* THE COVER-UPS, OR FORCING MYSELF TO EXPLORE SOMETHING I HATED? C'MON, I WAS SCARED! IT'S NOT LIKE I COULD PRETEND MY HORMONES DIDN'T EXIST!

FEH. TRY BEING A GIRL; THAT'S STANDARD PROCEDURE, UNLESS WE WANT TO BE LABELLED A "SLUT."

HEY, DON'T BLAME ME FOR THE WORLD'S DOUBLE STANDARDS.

I'M NOT; JUST DON'T TELL ME THE EASY WAY WAS THE ONLY WAY.

GREAT... THEN WE SHOULD EITHER BE OUT, OR... ASEXUAL?!

IS IT THAT HARD TO PICK AN OPTION THAT ISN'T MISLEADING?

FINE. DO YOU PLAN TO OUT EVERY GAY GUY IN THE WORLD, OR ONLY THE CLOSET CASES I HAPPEN TO SNOG?

YOU'RE THE RISK-TAKER... WHY NOT FIND OUT? BUT YOU'D ALL HAVE NOTHING TO FEAR IF YOU'D JUST BE HONEST ABOUT IT. TO BOTH YOURSELVES, AND OTHERS.

94

I'M ACTUALLY KINDA DISTURBED THAT SHE GUESSED YOU WERE GAY BEFORE I DID. SURE, I DO CHASE BIGGER GUYS, AND SHE'D EXPECT YOU TO BE MY TYPE, BUT...

WAIT...SO YOU KNEW SHE WAS ON TO ME FROM THE GET-GO?

ER, YEAH... AND YOU ARE KIND OF A PRIME TARGET FOR HER, WHAT WITH USING SAM FOR A FRONT, AND ALL THAT.

SO THAT'S WHY YOU'VE BEEN COUNSELING ME ALL THIS TIME? YOU HOPED I'D COME OUT AND IT'D RUIN HER PLANS?

NO, NO, THAT NEVER CROSSED MY MIND. ALL I EVER WANTED WAS YOU TO BE COMFORTABLE WITH YOURSELF.

EVERYTHING ELSE WAS SECONDARY.

HEH, SORRY. ALRIGHT THEN, SO WHAT DO WE DO NOW?

"WE"? NOTHING. THIS IS SOMETHING I HAVE TO DEAL WITH ON MY OWN.

PERHAPS SHE'LL SIMPLY GROW TIRED OF THE GAME EVENTUALLY. SHE'S GOTTA BELIEVE WE'RE EVEN SOMETIME.

BUT--

CODY, I DON'T WANT YOU TO GET INVOLVED ANY FURTHER. SHE'S JUST...TOO GOOD.

SHE'S BEEN ONE STEP AHEAD OF ME THIS WHOLE TIME. I DON'T KNOW HOW SHE DOES IT.

D'YOU THINK SHE'S RECRUITED SPIES?

DOUBTFUL. WHO'D BE SICK ENOUGH TO HELP HER WITH THIS?

95

I.S.O. NUMBER 9, JANUARY 2010, COPYRIGHT © VINCE SUZUKAWA. ALL RIGHTS RESERVED
THE STORIES, CHARACTERS, AND INCIDENTS MENTIONED IN THIS PUBLICATION ARE ENTIRELY FICTIONAL
PORTIONS OF THIS BOOK MAY BE REPRODUCED FOR PURPOSES OF REVIEW OR ADVERTISEMENT

YOU KNOW 'OW THE THIRD FLOOR DOESN'T RUN THE ENTIAH LENGTH OF THE BUILDING? AND IT 'AS A DOOR THAT LEADS OUT ONTO THE ROOF OF THE SECOND FLOOR?

I'VE SEEN THAT DOOR. I FIGURED IT'S FOR MAINTENANCE.

RAIGHT. BUT YOU CAN SEE THE ROOF FROM THE OTHAH 'ALLS IN THIS COMPLEX, AND AI'VE NOTICED SOMEONE PROWLING 'ROUND UP THEAH AFTAH HOURS. AND THE WEIRD PART IS... AI THINK AI'VE SEEN 'EM SLIP INTO A SECOND DOOR!

WELL, YOU'VE 'EARD THE LEGEND 'OW PART OF THE FLOOR BURNT DOWN IN A FIRE, AND THEY SALVAGED THE REST OF THE ROOMS? BUT TH' ROOMS WERE STAGGAHED, SO IF THEY BLOCKED OFF A NEW WALL IN A STRAIGHT LAINE...

WHAT? HOW?

...IT MEANT THEY JUST CUT OFF HALF OF ONE OF THE OLD ROOMS?

BINGO! AND THEAH'S NO ENTRANCE TO THAUT HALF-ROOM FROM THE INSAIDE, SO MAI GUESS IS YOU CAN ONLEH ENTER FROM THE OUTSAIDE ROOF.

*BEFORE*

*AFTER*

COULD JUST BE A STORAGE ROOM, THEN?

YEAH, BUT NOBODY SHOULD BE STOCKING TOILET PAPEH AT THAT TAIME O' DAY.

YOU... THINK IT COULD BE THE SPY, THEN?

POSSIBLY. THEY LOOK KAINDA SNEAKY. AND IT'S A GOOD VANTAGE POINT.

HM. THEY COULD SEE WHEN I MEET UP WITH JEFF. THEY MIGHT BE ABLE TO OVERHEAR WITH THE RIGHT EQUIPMENT. MAYBE EVEN RUN A WIRE TAP TO OUR ROOM!

YER GETTIN' CARRIED AWAY, MAITE.

HEH, OKAY.

I GUESS I NEVER LOOK AT OUR DORM THAT WAY. WHAT ARE YOU DOING ALL EVENING IN THE TOP FLOORS OF THE OTHER HAL--

STUPID, STUPID QUESTION.

SORREH!

98

I WONDER IF I COULD SNEAK A LADDER UP HERE. NAH, I'VE HEARD THE R.A. IS PRETTY ANAL. I'M PROBABLY PRESSING MY LUCK AS IT IS; I SHOULD GET A MOVE ON.

GONNA NEED ALL THE HELP I CAN GET. BETTER DITCH THE SHOES AND SHIRT.

CRAP. EVEN IF I GET BEYOND THIS, IT'S STILL GONNA BE A STRETCH.

I NEED MOMENTUM. WHICH I CAN'T GET WITHOUT ANOTHER FOOTHOLD...

HMM...

THAT JUST MIGHT WORK...

HOKAY THEN... I MUST NOT DIE A VIRGIN, I MUST NOT DIE A VIRGIN, I MUST NOT DIE A VIRGIN...

WHEW! NOT GONNA DIE A VIRGIN.

IT'S LIKE THIS PLACE WAS BUILT FOR YOU. THERE'S EVEN NATURAL LIGHTING.

YEAH, THE SKYLIGHT WAS CHEAPER THAN FIXING THE CEILING, THEY DISCOVERED.

I'M SURPRISED NO ONE ELSE CLAIMED IT.

WELL, IT WAS INTENDED TO BE STORAGE. BUT MOST OF THE STAFF CONSIDERS THIS FLOOR CURSED. SEEMS A LOT OF... INCIDENTS HAPPEN TO THIS DORM. SO NOBODY LIKES COMING HERE, AND IT'S BEEN ABANDONED FOR AWHILE.

THERE. THAT'S BETTER.

IN CASE OF FIRE DO NOT USE ELEVATORS

IN CASE OF COUCH DO NOT USE STAIRS

IN CASE OF GIANT DEADLY ESCAPED LAB ARMY ANTS...UM... YOU'RE ON YOUR OWN

COOL. AND I'LL BET THEY GIVE YOU A GREAT DISCOUNT ON THE RENT, HUH?

YEAH...OF COURSE.

UNLESS... THEY DON'T KNOW ABOUT YOU USING IT.

SIGH

THEY HAVEN'T EXACTLY NOMINATED ME FOR EMPLOYEE OF THE MONTH EVER SINCE THE FIRE. I DIDN'T THINK THEY'D APPROVE, SO I JUST MOVED IN HERE OVER THE BREAK.

YOU'RE NOT GOING TO...TELL ANYONE ABOUT THIS, ARE YOU?

COME ON. DO I LOOK LIKE THE SNITCHING TYPE?

SEEING AS HOW I'M NOT REALLY SUPPOSED TO BE HERE EITHER. AHEH...

YES... HOW LONG DID YOU THINK I WAS GOING TO LET THAT SLIDE?

104

JUST WHEN I WAS STARTING TO THINK YOU MIGHT NOT BE A COMPLETE BASTARD AFTER ALL. WHY THE HELL ARE YOU ASSOCIATING WITH THAT...THAT--

NOW HOLD UP. YOU DON'T KNOW HER.

HAVE YOU EVEN MET HER? I'VE SEEN HER TAKE DOWN DRUNK DRIVERS, DEADBEAT SPOUSES, EMBEZZLERS, ALMOST DAILY. SHE'S NO MONSTER.

YEAH, YEAH. SO...WHAT HAPPENS IF SHE GETS ASSIGNED TO A GAY HATE CRIME CASE, HUH?

I SWEAR, THAT ISN'T THE ISSUE. SHE'S NOT HOMOPHOBIC. AND NEITHER AM I.

RIGHT, YOU'RE BOTH JUST TWO PEAS IN A POD. SO HOW DID YOU GET SUCKED INTO THIS MESS, THEN? WHAT'D SHE OFFER YOU?

NOTHING.

NOTHING? AS IF.

REALLY.

SHE ONLY APPROACHED ME SINCE I WORK NEAR JEFF. I THOUGHT IT WAS SOME SILLY SIBLING RIVALRY GAME.

BUT, I FIGURED I'D NEED LEGAL ADVICE ON MY DEBT WITH THE SCHOOL AT SOME POINT. SO I DID IT AS A FAVOR... AT FIRST.

AND I WON'T LIE. I'D WATCHED JEFF ANONYMOUSLY PLAYING PRANKS ON STUDENTS WHO'D CAUSED EXCESS REPAIRS. I THOUGHT HE WAS COWARDLY AND IMMATURE. I DIDN'T NEED MUCH PERSUADING.

AND WHAT WAS YOUR BEEF WITH ME?

DO NOT WALK ON THE GRASS OR ELSE

OH...RIGHT. UM, WE WEREN'T EXACTLY WINNING POINTS WITH EACH OTHER FROM THE GET-GO, WERE WE?

NOPE.

105

UNBELIEVABLE. SO...WHAT KIND OF BLACKMAIL DID YOU HAVE IN STORE FOR *ME*, HUH?

C'MON, I'M NOT PROUD OF WHAT I DID. BUT I ONLY AGREED TO SPY ON YOU TO SEE HOW FAR YOU WERE GETTING ON WITH JEFF.

MM-HM. AND WHAT ABOUT OUR LITTLE CONFRONTATIONS AT THE HANGOUT, HUH?

ER, OKAY, I ADMIT, THE FIRST TIME IT WAS ALL ME. BUT THE NEXT TIME, MAUREEN SUGGESTED I PICK A FIGHT--AND LET YOU WIN.

SO WHAT ABOUT JEREMY? WHAT GAVE YOU THE RIGHT TO RUIN HIS LIFE?

SIGH...IT'S JUST...REENA, ER, MAUREEN CAN BE PRETTY PERSUASIVE. SHE SAID WE WERE ONLY SPEEDING UP THE INEVITABLE.

YOU WERE SUPPOSED TO BE THE HERO. SHE WANTED TO SHOW THAT YOU DIDN'T NEED JEFF'S HELP TO HOOK UP WITH DOUG. BUT, WELL, THEN YOUR BUDDY INTERFERED...

I DOUBT JEFF WAS GIVING YOU THE FULL STORY. I MEAN, DO YOU HONESTLY THINK JEREMY'S PARENTS WOULD SIMPLY ACCEPT PHOTOS FROM A TOTAL STRANGER?

THEY ACTUALLY HAD SUSPECTED ALL ALONG...JEFF WASN'T VERY DISCREET. MAYBE HE SHOULD'VE BEEN THINKING OF JEREMY'S LIVING SITUATION FIRST, RATHER THAN SEX.

PLUS I'D ALREADY ASKED DOUG ANYWAY.

YEAH... WE HAD NO IDEA.

THE POINT IS, IT WAS NOTHING PERSONAL AGAINST YOU, OR DOUG. IF IT'D WORKED OUT RIGHT, SHE MIGHT HAVE NEVER BOTHERED YOU AGAIN.

WHY DIDN'T HE JUST WAIT A YEAR FOR JEREMY TO GRADUATE AND MOVE OUT?

THAT'S NOT FOR HER TO JUDGE. DON'T YOU HAVE A MIND OF YOUR OWN?

I COULDN'T HELP IT; I WAS IN TOO DEEP AT THAT POINT.

AW, POOR BABY. GUESS SHE REALLY MUSTA HAD YOU BY THE--

LOOK, I... I'M IN LOVE!

WHOA, I DIDN'T MEAN *LITERALLY*! SO IS PSYCHO-BITCHAPHILIA THE NEW FETISH THESE DAYS?

YOU'RE TREADING ON DANGEROUS GROUND, KID.

108

109

YER ABSOLUTELY RAIGHT, BORIS...AI SHOULD TELL ZACH THAT AI-- OI, CODY!

MUNCH MUNCH

HEY GUYS, SORRY THAT TOOK SO LONG.

SO WOT WAS IN THEAH? DEAD BODIES? ELVIS? THE LOST CITY OF ATLANTIS?

YEAH, ABOUT THAT...

HUH... IT'S NOT MY POSITION TO SAY ANYTHING ABOUT THOR'S SITUATION...

IT WAS JUST... STORAGE.

STORAGE?! YOU WERE THERE ALL THAUT TAIME FOAH STORAGE?

'FRAID SO.

STRANGE, THOUGH...THOR SURE SEEMED EAGAH TO GET 'IS ARSE IN THEAH...

WEIRD. UH...MAYBE HE WANTED OUT THERE FOR A SMOKE?

P'RHAPS. YA SHOULDA SEEN 'IM...POLAITE AS ANYTHING, BUT JUST HOISTED ME CLEAR OUTTA THE WAY.

COME T' THINK OF IT, MAITE, 'E MAKES A BETTAH BOUNCAH THAN YOU DO!

BETTER? AS IF! I COULDA TAKEN HIM OFF IF I'D BEEN THERE...

NAUT FROM WOT AI'VE SEEN.

WHAT'S THAT SUPPOSED TO-- HEY!

NO! NO! QUIT IT!

AHAHAHAHA!

WOT, ME, BITTAH 'BOUT YOU LEAVIN' US TO WORRY ALL THIS TIME? NAUT AT ALL! BORIS, HOLD DOWN AN ARM, WILLYA?

MUNCH MUNCH

I'M SORRY, I'M SORRY!!

WAAAHAHAA!

110

# iSO CHAPTER 18
## FIRE AND EYESORE

THE NEXT DAY AT THE HANGOUT

SIGH

CODY, CAN I SEE YOU IN MY OFFICE FOR A SEC?

YAAAH! YES'M.

THIS IS WHERE YOU FIRE ME, ISN'T IT? I FIGURED THIS WAS COMING. I DON'T BLAME YOU, I'LL BET YOU ALL HATE ME NOW.

NOT AT ALL, CODY. NOBODY HATES YOU.

I MEAN... I WAS FINALLY WARMING UP TO YOU, AND I HOPE IT MIGHT WORK OUT...BUT IF NOT, THEN I GUESS IT'S FOR THE BEST. THE THING IS...HONESTLY, IT WAS GOOD FOR DOUG... DO YOU KNOW THIS IS THE FIRST RELATIONSHIP HE'S HAD THAT ENDED NORMALLY? HE DIDN'T GET SCREAMED AT, STOLEN FROM, OR TOTALLY ABANDONED. YOU TWO JUST SAT DOWN, AND TALKED IT OUT. MINIMAL DRAMA.

FOR ONCE, IT DIDN'T END IN A HURRY SIMPLY BECAUSE HE WAS DATING A FREAK. HE HAD TO SHARE SOME OF THE RESPONSIBILITY, AND... Y'KNOW, LOOK INSIDE HIMSELF THIS TIME. AND I THINK HE'S LEARNED FROM IT.

SO I REALIZE IT COULD BE A LITTLE AWKWARD AROUND HERE FOR A BIT, BUT I WANTED TO REASSURE YOU THAT WE'RE NOT GOING TO SHOVE YOU OUT THE DOOR. OKAY?

WELL, THANKS... BUT ACTUALLY...I WAS GOING TO TELL YOU I'M PLANNING TO QUIT AT THE END OF THE SEMESTER.

OH.

...SO, YEAH, BETWEEN THE AWKWARDNESS, AND, ER, MY, GPA--

I'LL ASK AROUND.

RANDALL MIGHT BE INTERESTED. HE'S KINDA BIG, NOT A PUSHOVER, KICKS ASS AT HOCKEY...

'E MAKES A BETTAH BOUNCAH THAN YOU DO!

I UNDERSTAND. THANKS FOR GIVING US PLENTY OF NOTICE...

WE CAN FIND SOMEONE BEFORE WINTER BREAK NOW.

WAIT, HE'S UNDERAGE, TOO. BETTER NOT RISK THAT.

WHO ELSE DO I KNOW THAT'S--

NO... THAT'S CRAZY.

AND YET...IT WORKS. THOR'S QUALIFIED. AND HE WANTS A JOB THAT ISN'T THROUGH THE SCHOOL, AND WHERE HE'LL GET A LITTLE RESPECT. IF TYRONE CAN GIVE HIM A BETTER PAYMENT PLAN, HE MAY FEEL LESS LIKE A SLAVE.

PLUS, IT'S A NIGHT JOB. HE COULD DO THE PARENTING THANG, AND KEEP WORKING...

THEN NOBODY COULD ACCUSE HIM OF GOLD-DIGGING.

SAY, SAM? TYRONE'S STILL WINNING ALL THOSE BARTENDING COMPETITIONS, RIGHT?

OH, HECK YEAH.

I KEEP TELLING HIM HE SHOULD INVEST SOMEWHERE, BUT HE'S SO PARANOID ABOUT THAT RIGHT NOW.

WHY DO YOU ASK?

WELL...

ARE YOU OUT OF YOUR FREAKIN' MIND???

WHOA!

RUN AWAY, RUN AWAY!

TYRONE?

MEETING!!

GO WING SOMEWHERE ΦΛΥ

GO WING SOMEWHERE ΦΛΥ

THE HANG

112

LOOK, THERE'S A MULTITUDE OF REASONS I COULD GIVE...NO, I HAVE TO BE HONEST, MOST OF THEM WERE JUST EXCUSES. AND WHETHER THEY MADE ANY MORE SENSE TO ME AT THE TIME THAN THEY DO NOW IS IRRELEVANT. I FIGURED AS LONG AS NOBODY ACTUALLY GOT INJURED, IT WAS OKAY, AND I ALMOST SUCCEEDED THERE.

SO I'LL JUST SAY IT: I WAS AN IDIOT. A TOTAL AND COMPLETE IDIOT, AND I'M SORRY.

I HAD SOMETHING TO PROVE, FOR A REASON THAT NO LONGER EXISTS, AND I WAS COWARDLY FOR NOT COMING BACK HERE AS SOON AS IT DIDN'T.

I APOLOGIZE FOR ALL THE TROUBLE AND AGGRAVATION I CAUSED. IT WON'T HAPPEN AGAIN.

UH, DON'T MENTION IT.

THANKS, MAN.

PSSST...THINK YOU COULD...COME BACK A FEW MORE TIMES? MAYBE GIVE SOME EXTRA TIPS?

MIGHT PROVE YOU REALLY MEANT IT.

WELL....I SUPPOSE.

OVER THE COURSE OF THE NEXT WEEK...

...

...

...

...

YOU SURE IT'S A GOOD IDEA TO KEEP COMING BACK? I DON'T THINK SAM WANTS ME HERE.

EH, SHE'LL BE ALRIGHT.

PLUS, AREN'T YOU SICK OF TASTING MY DRINK FIRST?

YEAH, KINDA.

114

115

BEEP BEEP BEEP BEEP

WHA?

THAT'S THE SMOKE DETECTOR!

BEEP
BEEP
BEEP
BEEP

BEEP

OOF!

HEY, IT'S COMIN' FROM THE MEN'S ROOM!

JUST CALM DOWN, AND WATCH YOUR STEP. THERE'S NO REASON TO PANIC.

SORRY, MAN...

BEEP

YOU HEAR THAT?

LET'S GET OUTTA HERE!

BEEP

BEEP
BEEP

BEEP

ARE YOU ALL RIGHT?

YEAH, THANKS.

I THINK THAT'S EVERYONE. YOU CALLING 911, SAM?

BEEP
BEEP
BEEP

YEAH! BUT HAVE YOU SEEN DOUG?

BEEP BEEP BEEP BEEP BEEP

118

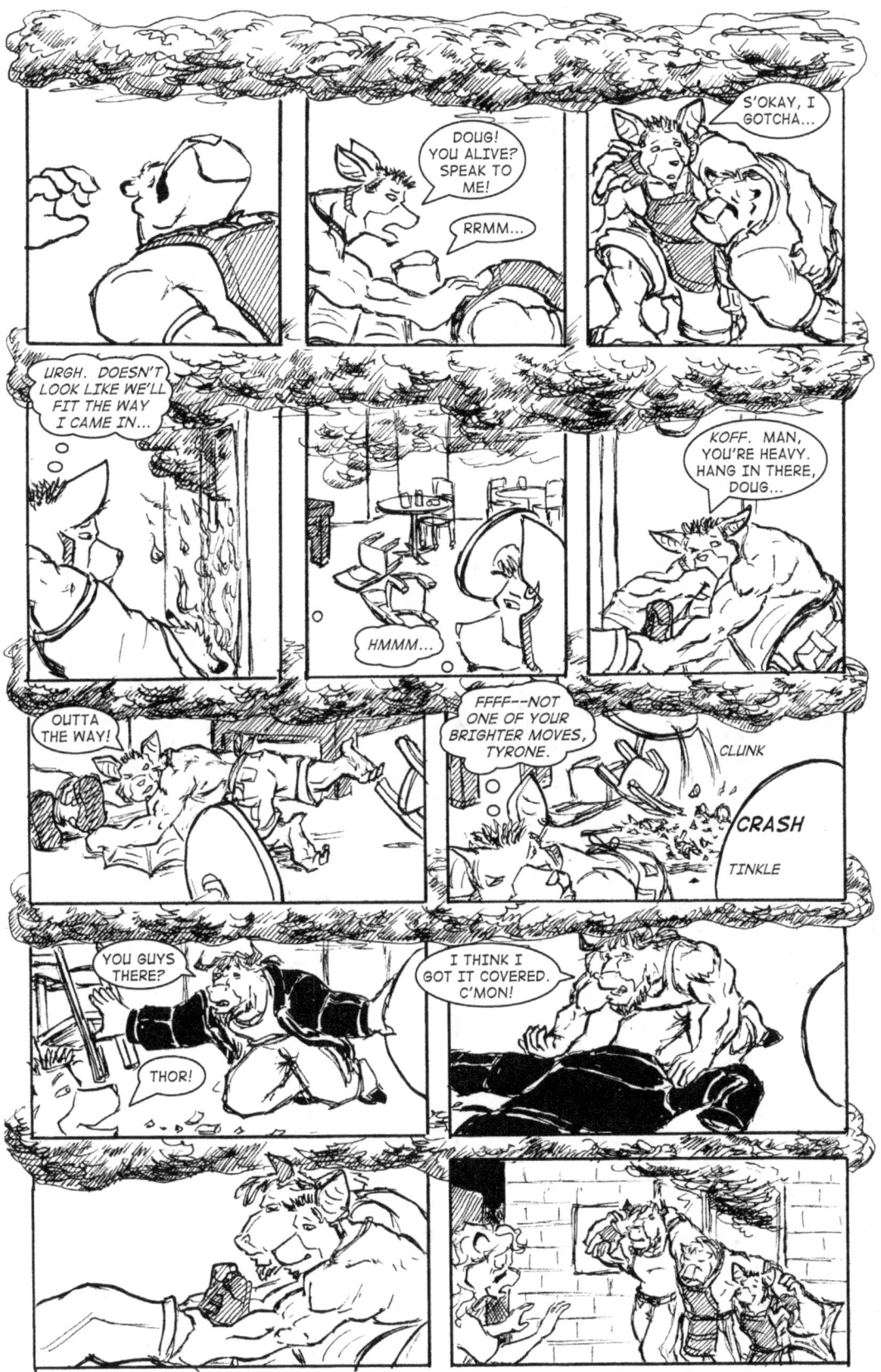

WHERE IS EVERYO-- BECKY! HOW BAD WAS IT?

JUST CALM DOWN. DOUG, TY, AND THOR ARE AT THE HOSPITAL, BUT THEY'RE ALL GONNA BE FINE. SAM WENT WITH THEM, AND I STAYED BEHIND TO FILE THE REPORT.

HOW...HOW'D IT HAPPEN?

THEY'RE STILL CHECKING, BUT IT LOOKS LIKE IT WAS STARTED BY DOUG'S EX...

WHAT?! WHY THAT...HE'S LUCKY HE'S IN CUSTODY, OTHERWISE I'D--

YEAH, YOU AND SAM BOTH. BUT WORD OF ADVICE, LET'S NOT MAKE DEATH THREATS WHILE THE POLICE ARE STILL AROUND, HMM?

125

127

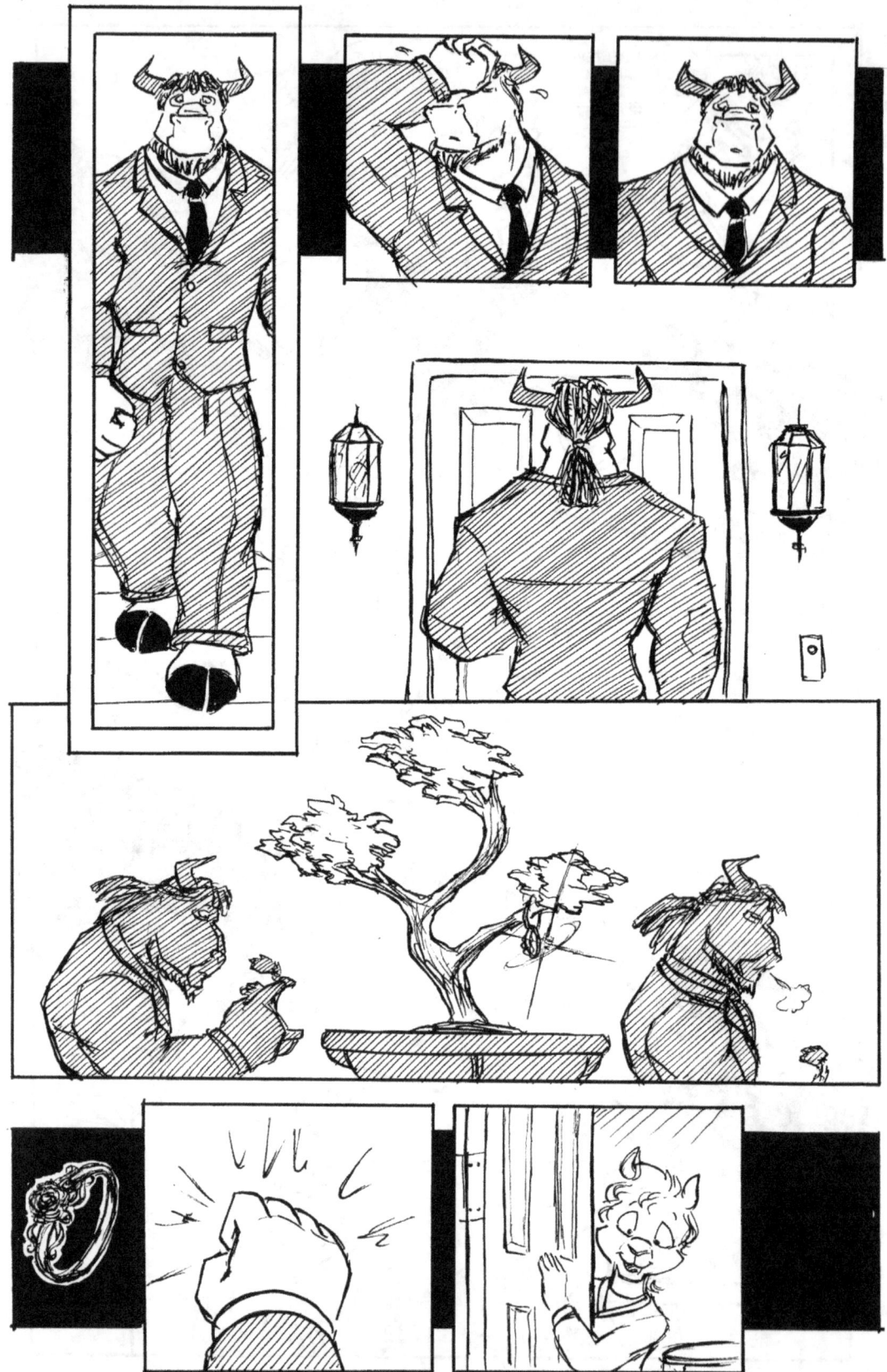

# CHAPTER 19

## IS ONLY THE BEGINNING

ART & STORY BY VINCE SUZUKAWA

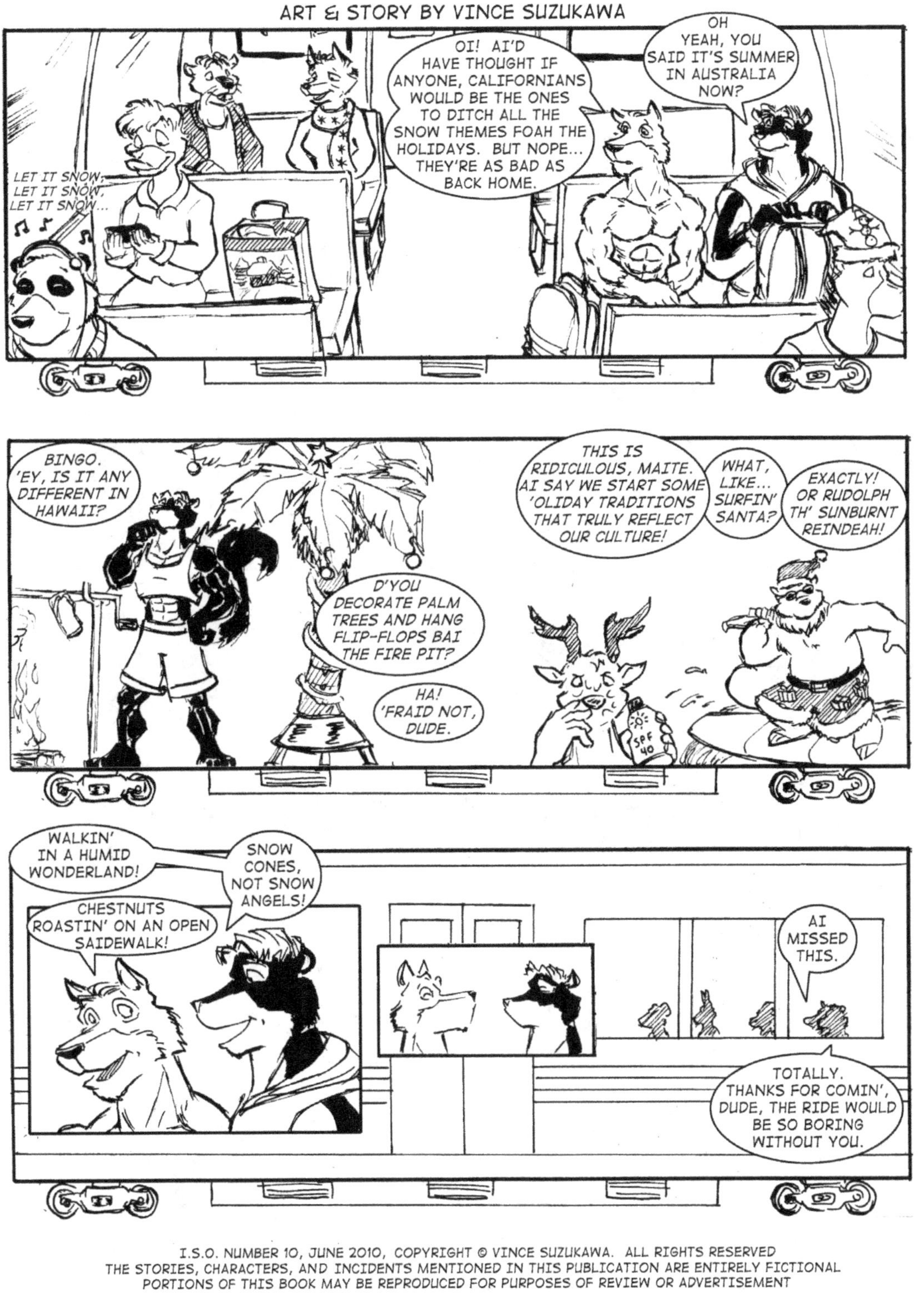

I.S.O. NUMBER 10, JUNE 2010, COPYRIGHT © VINCE SUZUKAWA. ALL RIGHTS RESERVED
THE STORIES, CHARACTERS, AND INCIDENTS MENTIONED IN THIS PUBLICATION ARE ENTIRELY FICTIONAL
PORTIONS OF THIS BOOK MAY BE REPRODUCED FOR PURPOSES OF REVIEW OR ADVERTISEMENT

130

OH, MAN. DUDE, THIS IS...LIKE, KINDA WHY I HAD NO IDEA YOU WERE SERIOUSLY AFTER ME, Y'KNOW?

YEAH... S'POSE AI REALLY CAN'T BLAME YA.

IT'S LIKE ALWAYS *ON* WITH YOU! HOW DO YOU SHOW ANYONE THAT YOU'RE REALLY INTERESTED IN THEM?

AI...NEVER REALLY THOUGHT ABOUT IT.

BUT YOU'RE TOTALLY RAIGHT, THOUGH.

SO THAUT'S WHY AI...HM, EASIEST IF AI SHOW YA. S'KAINDA EARLY, BUT, MERREH CHRISTMAS!

HEH, THAT'S COOL, THANKS! MAYBE I CAN WEAR IT TO THE PARTY!

CAUGHT IN A RAD BROMANCE

CAUGHT IN A RAD BROMANCE

OH, NO NO NO, IT'S NAUT FOAH *YOU*, MAITE...

131

I HOPE YOU GOT PLENTY OF REST... WE'LL BE SHOOTING ALL NIGHT.

AI'M GOOD. CRAIKEY, S'A LOT GOIN' ON.

THEY'RE USUALLY CLOSED FOR MAINTENANCE JUST BEFORE THE HOLIDAYS. IT WAS THE PERFECT TIME TO RENT IT.

OI, WE 'AVE THE 'OLE PLAICE T' OURSELVES?

YUP!

AI ESPECIALLY LOVED YER PERFORMANCE DURING WEEK TEN. EVEN MAI ROOMIE WAS IMPRESSED, AND 'E 'ATES DIANE SALINAS! UH...AI THINK.

ANYWAY, YOU KNOW ELLIS ALREADY. BUT I'D LIKE YOU TO MEET--

OI, NO INTRODUCTION NECESSARY! MS BROWN, AI'M JAKE.

NICE TO MEET YOU.

BUT PLEASE-- CALL ME JAMIE!

WHY THANK YOU, THAT'S SO SWEET... Y'KNOW, YOU'RE A LOT NICER THAN THE LAST DANCER WE HAD.

OH? WOT DID 'E DO?

HEY, LOOK AT THE TIME...C'MON, YOU'VE GOT A TON OF REHEARSING TO DO.

SEE YOU SOON!

BAI!

OOH. FLUFFY. GOOD THING TOO, YOU MAY NEED IT.

OI?

YEAH, YOU'LL HAVE TO LOSE THE SHIRT FOR SOME OF THE SHOTS. MIGHT GET COLD!

D'OH!

135

OOOH, THAT'S GOING TO BE YOUR NEXT SINGLE? COOL!

YUP! OH HEY, YOU CAN FOLLOW ME ON NATTER, I MAKE ANNOUNCEMENTS LIKE THAT ALL THE TIME. I'M ON AS "BIGBROWNEYES."

WILL DO!

SO, I UH, HOPE MY COUSIN WASN'T TOO MUCH OF A HANDFUL FOR YA?

NO, NOT AT ALL! IN FACT, HE WAS A COMPLETE GENTLEMAN...

UNLIKE THAT OTHER CREEP THEY HIRED.

HE WAS?!

ACTUALLY, I LOVED WORKING WITH HIM SO MUCH, I'VE ASKED HIM TO BE A BACKUP DANCER FOR MY TOUR THIS SUMMER.

SERIOUSLY? HE MUST BE THRILLED! WHERE IS HE?

I THINK HE'S STILL IN WARDROBE--OH, THERE HE IS!

WHUMP

JAKE! WE JUST HEARD!

CONGRATULATIONS!

YOUR BIG BREAK...

I'M SO HAPPY FOR YOU!

SEE THE WORLD

...LY EXCIT...

...H FUN!

THIS MUST BE LIKE A DREAM COME TRUE, EH?

UH... JAKE?

AWW, THE POOR THING! HE WAS GOING FULL STEAM ALL NIGHT, HE MUST BE EXHAUSTED.

THAT'S WEIRD; USUALLY HE HAS NO TROUBLE--OOF! HEY!

ZZZZZZZ...

YOU SURE I SHOULD BE HERE FOR THIS?

MAUREEN SAID SHE'D LIKE TO TALK TO YOU TOO. JUST HANG TIGHT IN HERE, OKAY?

I WONDER HOW IT'S GOING IN THERE..

SO...I DON'T EVEN KNOW WHERE TO BEGIN.

"SORRY" MIGHT BE A GOOD PLACE. GOT PLENTY OF OTHER SUGGESTIONS, IF YOU NEED 'EM.

FAIR ENOUGH... I'M SORRY. I'M SURE YOU CAN UNDERSTAND WHY I WASN'T THINKING CLEARLY AFTER EVERYTHING... IMPLODED. BUT, I SHOULDN'T HAVE TAKEN IT OUT ON YOU.

YES, I KNOW... I LASHED OUT. BUT I WASN'T GOING TO KEEP IT UP FOREVER. JUST--

I'LL SAY. OKAY, I HAD A MOMENT OF WEAKNESS, AND IT SURE AS HELL TAUGHT ME TO NEVER GET THAT DRUNK *EVER* AGAIN. BUT HOW WAS I TO KNOW IT'D TURN OUT THAT WAY?

JUST WHAT? JUST LONG ENOUGH TO RUIN SOMEONE ELSE'S LIFE?

OR... MAYBE ABOUT AS LONG AS YOU WERE PLANNING TO STAY IN THE CLOSET FROM US?

LEMME GUESS, WAS IT GOING TO BE AN EYE FOR AN EYE, AND GO ON AS LONG AS YOU WERE DATING WENDELL?

· · ·

TOUCHÉ.

140

OKAY, I ADMIT I WAS FURIOUS AT FIRST.

CAN YOU BLAME ME?

YES, I WAS AVOIDING YOUR CALLS; I COULDN'T DEAL THE FINAL BLOW OVER THE PHONE.

I KNEW IF I COULDN'T DO IT WITHOUT LOOKING YOU IN THE EYE, THEN I WAS IN THE WRONG.

SO I CAME BY ONE EVENING AND... THAT'S WHEN I SAW HIM.

JEREMY?

YES. YOUR... BOYFRIEND.

IT WAS SOON QUITE CLEAR HE WAS NO ONE-NIGHT FLING... THIS WAS SOMEONE YOU KNEW WELL... FOR MONTHS, PROBABLY.

JEFF, YOU'D... CREATED ANOTHER WHOLE LIFE FOR YOURSELF. WE'D NEVER BEEN PARTICULARLY CLOSE, BUT I COULDN'T BELIEVE THAT MUCH HAD GONE UNDER MY RADAR.

I REALIZED I BARELY KNEW YOU, AND IT WAS A SLAP IN THE FACE BECAUSE YOU'D KEPT ME AT BAY ON PURPOSE.

YOU AT LEAST HAD MET WENDELL. I'D NEVER EVEN **HEARD** ABOUT THIS JEREMY. IF HE WAS SO IMPORTANT TO YOU, I WOULD'VE WANTED TO KNOW.

MOM AND DAD WOULD'VE WANTED TO KNOW.

C'MON, I WAS STILL FIGURING THINGS OUT WHEN THEY DIED.

BUT YOU HAD AT LEAST SUSPECTED YOU LIKED GUYS FOR AWHILE, RIGHT?

I...

...DID, YES.

142

I MISSED THIS, JEFF. AGE GAP AND ALL, YOU'VE ALWAYS BEEN THERE.

WELL, I THINK WE'RE BACK ON TRACK NOW.

MAYBE I CAN REBUILD YOUR TRUST OVER CHRISTMAS DINNER...?

I'D LIKE THAT.

JUST... NO MORE SECRETS.

AND NO FRIENDS WITH SECRETS. PROVIDED THERE'S NO RUINING ANYONE'S LIVES?

RIGHT. JUST MAKE SURE THEY'RE NOT RUINING THEIR OWN LIVES THEMSELVES.

DEAL.

SPEAKING OF FRIENDS...DID YOU SAY CODY WAS HERE?

OH, YEAH. HE'S IN THE BACK.

YOUR PRESENCE IS REQUESTED, MY GOOD MAN.

GOTCHA.

CODY...I MUST APOLOGIZE FOR SPYING ON YOU TOO. WE... DIDN'T KNOW THE GOOD JEFF WAS DOING YOU, AND WE THOUGHT YOU WERE JUST PERPETUATING THE CYCLE. IF THERE'S ANYTHING I CAN DO TO MAKE UP FOR IT, PLEASE--

IT'S OKAY.

WHILE I, UH, CAN'T AGREE WITH YOUR METHODS, YOU KINDA HAD A RIGHT TO MAKE YOUR POINT. TO BOTH OF US.

OH?

JEFF, YOU'RE TOO SMART TO LET HER KEEP HARASSING YOU. I THINK ON SOME LEVEL, YOU AGREED WITH HER ENOUGH TO GUILT YOURSELF. MAYBE YOU FELT THIS CONTACT WITH HER WAS BETTER THAN NOTHING.

HEH. TOUCHE. BEEN PRACTICING YOUR PSYCHO-BABBLE?

A LITTLE! AS FOR ME...

SOUNDS LIKE A PRETTY STRENUOUS SCHEDULE TO ME.

OI, TELL ME 'BOUT IT. THANK GOODNESS YER WINT--UH, SUMMER BREAK IS LONGAH THAN OURS!

AND DUDE! I THINK JAMIE LIKES YOU!

SO JUST HOW TALL *IS* SHE IN REAL LIFE?

MUNCH

MUNCH

MUNCH

HAVE YOU MET THE NEW BOUNCER AT KYELL'S?

NOT YET. I'LL MISS FORRIN...I WAS HOPING TO GET HIM TO SMILE JUST ONCE BEFORE HE LEFT.

OH, I GUARANTEE I'LL PUT A SMILE ON THE NEW GUY'S FACE.

WHICH BOUQUET? WELL...WHAT SORT OF LADY ARE WE TALKING HERE?

HMM... SHE'S FEMININE, BUT NOT DELICATE. SHE LIKES RED... I THINK?

DID YOU HAVE ANOTHER FIGHT WITH KATHY?

YOU *HAVE* TO GET THE COLLECTORS' EDITION! THE COMMENTARY TRACK ALONE IS WORTH IT!

OOH, DIDJA FIND THE EASTER EGG ON THE SETUP MENU?

OKAY, OKAY, MAYBE NEXT PAYCHECK.

MAUREEN, IT'S ABSOLUTELY STUNNING! DON'T YOU AGREE, CODY?

WHY THANK YOU!

OOH!

ER... YEAH, IT'S... UH, PRETTY COOL.

WHA--DID YOU JUST CALL IT...?! SIGH... *MEN!*

147

148

# iSO

## CHAPTER 19.5

### IN SEARCH OF HIDDEN TREASURE

LOCATION: FORREST UNIVERSITY

FORREST DROIDS
VS
DEMONTFORT GRYPHONS

HOME 4    VISITOR 4

12:03

PERIOD 4

PLAYER PENALTY 3 | PLAYER PENALTY 6

THE GAME IS TIED.

THE RIVALRY BETWEEN THESE TWO SCHOOLS IS LEGENDARY...

WOOOOO!

GO RANDALL!

THE RINK IS NO EXCEPTION.

WINGER

BOOOOOOOOOOOOOOO!!!

ALONG WITH THE SPECTATORS...

SCHOOL SPIRIT IS IMPORTANT WHEN DEMONTFORT IS THE VISITING TEAM...SO NOTHING WOULD KEEP THEIR FRIENDS FROM SHOWING THEIR SUPPORT.

ALMOST NOTHING...

STORY & ADDITIONAL CHARACTERS - R. SMITH / CONCEPT & ART - VINCE SUZUKAWA

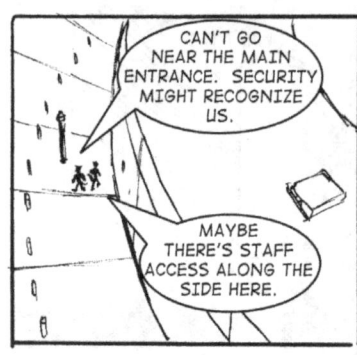

CAN'T GO NEAR THE MAIN ENTRANCE. SECURITY MIGHT RECOGNIZE US.

MAYBE THERE'S STAFF ACCESS ALONG THE SIDE HERE.

THINK THIS'LL DO?

WHY NOT?

BEEP

IF ANYONE ASKS, JUST SAY WE'RE HERE FOR ZAMBONI MAINTENANCE.

OR HOW ABOUT I DO THE TALKING INSTEAD?

BEEP

BEEP

BEEP

MMMAYBE YOU SHOULD LET ME CHOOSE THE DOORS, TOO.

IT'S ALL ABOUT YOU YOU YOU, ISN'T IT?

BEEP

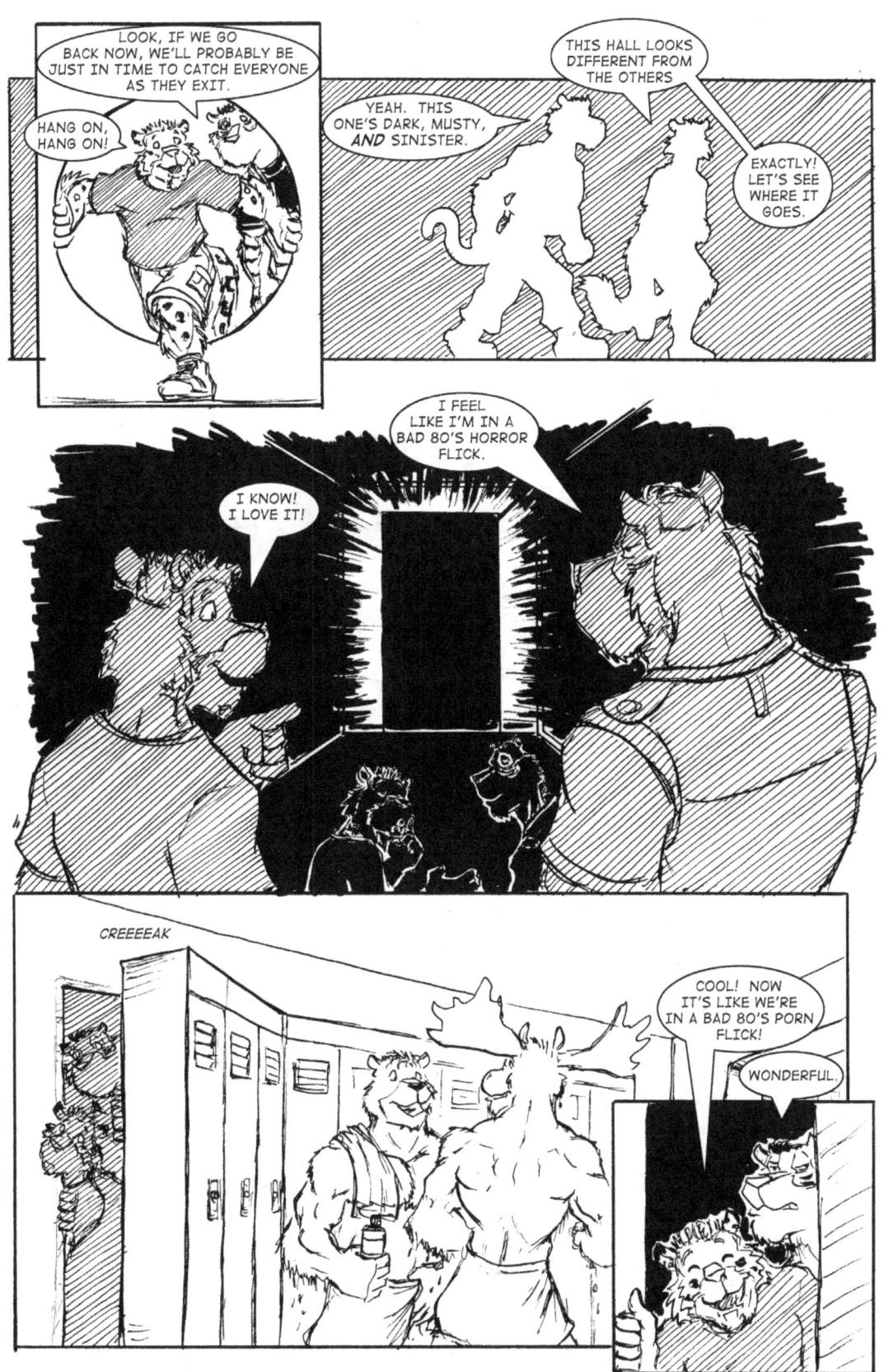

153

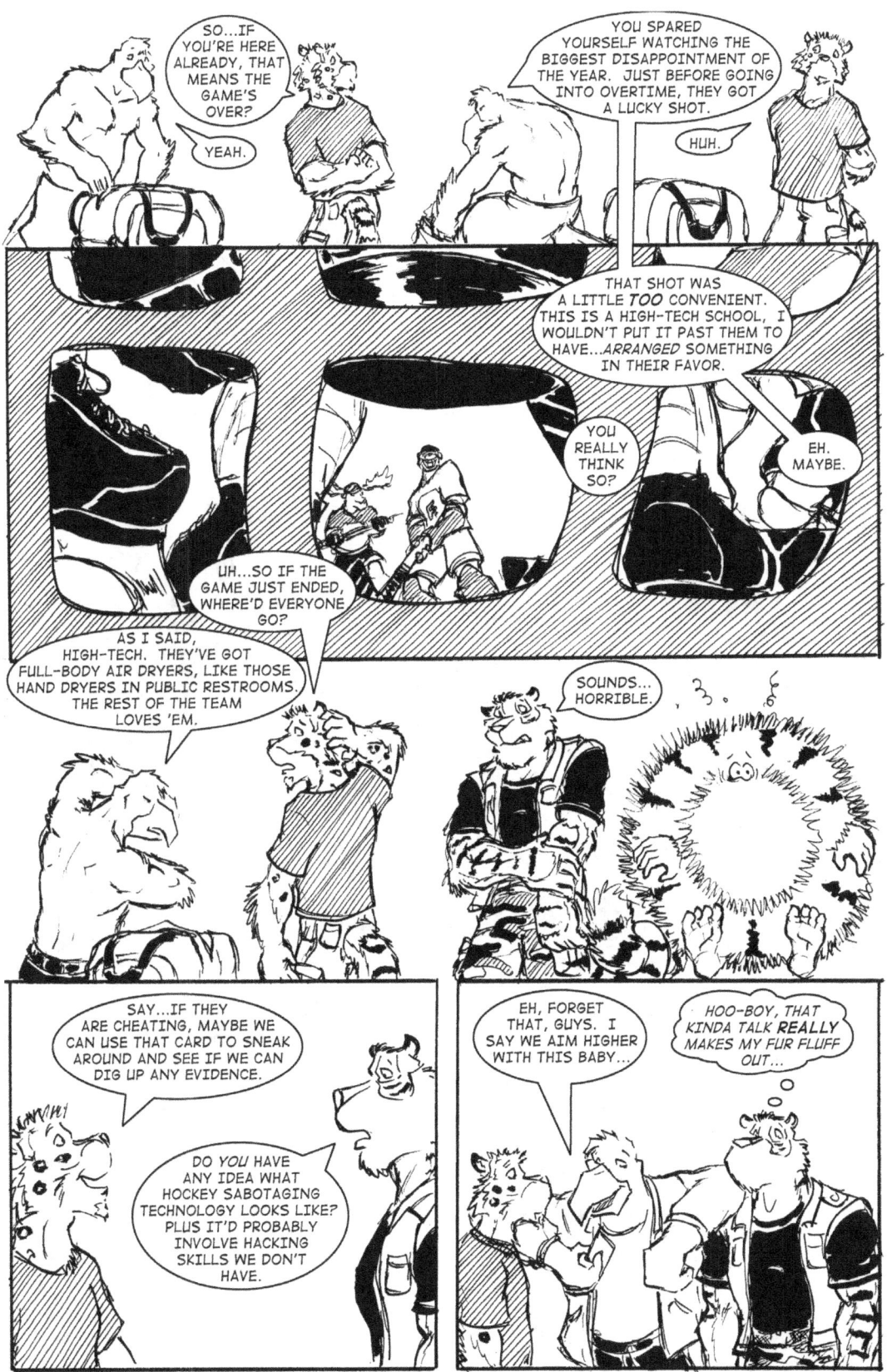

SO...IF YOU'RE HERE ALREADY, THAT MEANS THE GAME'S OVER?

YEAH.

YOU SPARED YOURSELF WATCHING THE BIGGEST DISAPPOINTMENT OF THE YEAR. JUST BEFORE GOING INTO OVERTIME, THEY GOT A LUCKY SHOT.

HUH.

THAT SHOT WAS A LITTLE *TOO* CONVENIENT. THIS IS A HIGH-TECH SCHOOL, I WOULDN'T PUT IT PAST THEM TO HAVE...*ARRANGED* SOMETHING IN THEIR FAVOR.

YOU REALLY THINK SO?

EH. MAYBE.

UH...SO IF THE GAME JUST ENDED, WHERE'D EVERYONE GO?

AS I SAID, HIGH-TECH. THEY'VE GOT FULL-BODY AIR DRYERS, LIKE THOSE HAND DRYERS IN PUBLIC RESTROOMS. THE REST OF THE TEAM LOVES 'EM.

SOUNDS... HORRIBLE.

SAY...IF THEY ARE CHEATING, MAYBE WE CAN USE THAT CARD TO SNEAK AROUND AND SEE IF WE CAN DIG UP ANY EVIDENCE.

DO *YOU* HAVE ANY IDEA WHAT HOCKEY SABOTAGING TECHNOLOGY LOOKS LIKE? PLUS IT'D PROBABLY INVOLVE HACKING SKILLS WE DON'T HAVE.

EH, FORGET THAT, GUYS. I SAY WE AIM HIGHER WITH THIS BABY...

HOO-BOY, THAT KINDA TALK *REALLY* MAKES MY FUR FLUFF OUT...

160

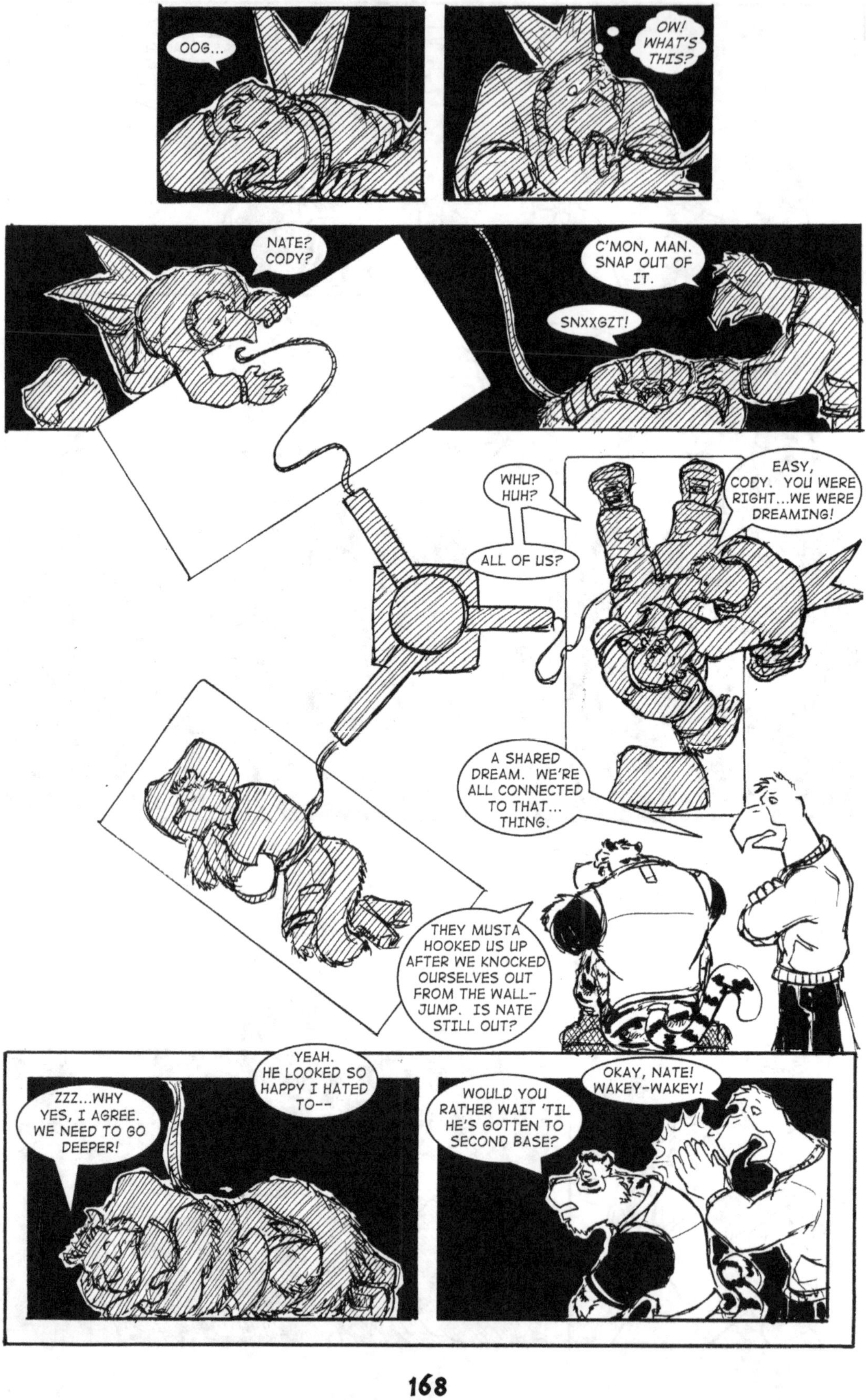

OOG...

OW! WHAT'S THIS?

NATE? CODY?

C'MON, MAN. SNAP OUT OF IT.

SNXXGZT!

WHU? HUH?

EASY, CODY. YOU WERE RIGHT...WE WERE DREAMING!

ALL OF US?

A SHARED DREAM. WE'RE ALL CONNECTED TO THAT... THING.

THEY MUSTA HOOKED US UP AFTER WE KNOCKED OURSELVES OUT FROM THE WALL-JUMP. IS NATE STILL OUT?

ZZZ...WHY YES, I AGREE. WE NEED TO GO DEEPER!

YEAH. HE LOOKED SO HAPPY I HATED TO--

WOULD YOU RATHER WAIT 'TIL HE'S GOTTEN TO SECOND BASE?

OKAY, NATE! WAKEY-WAKEY!

169

170

172

173

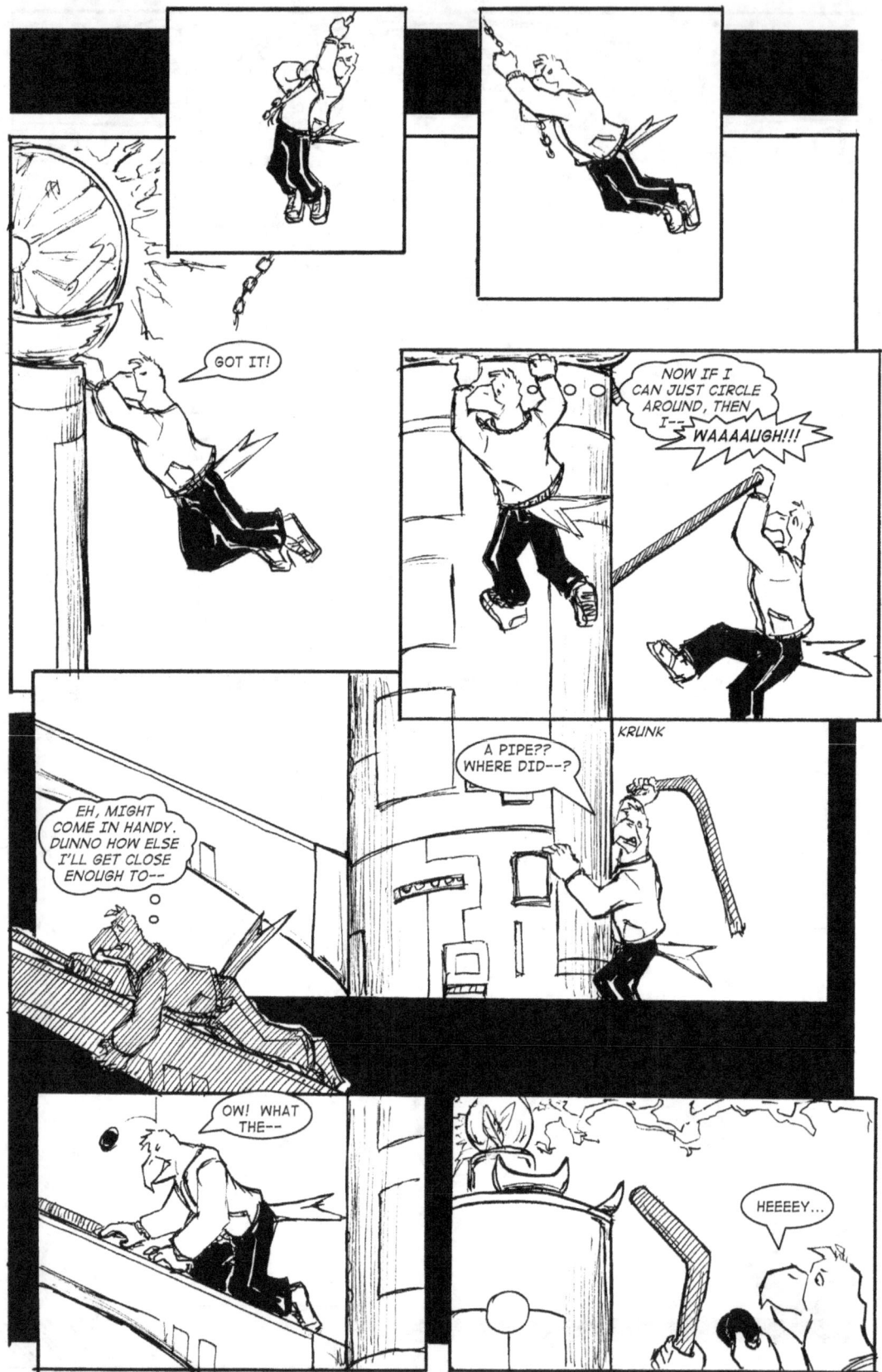

176

177

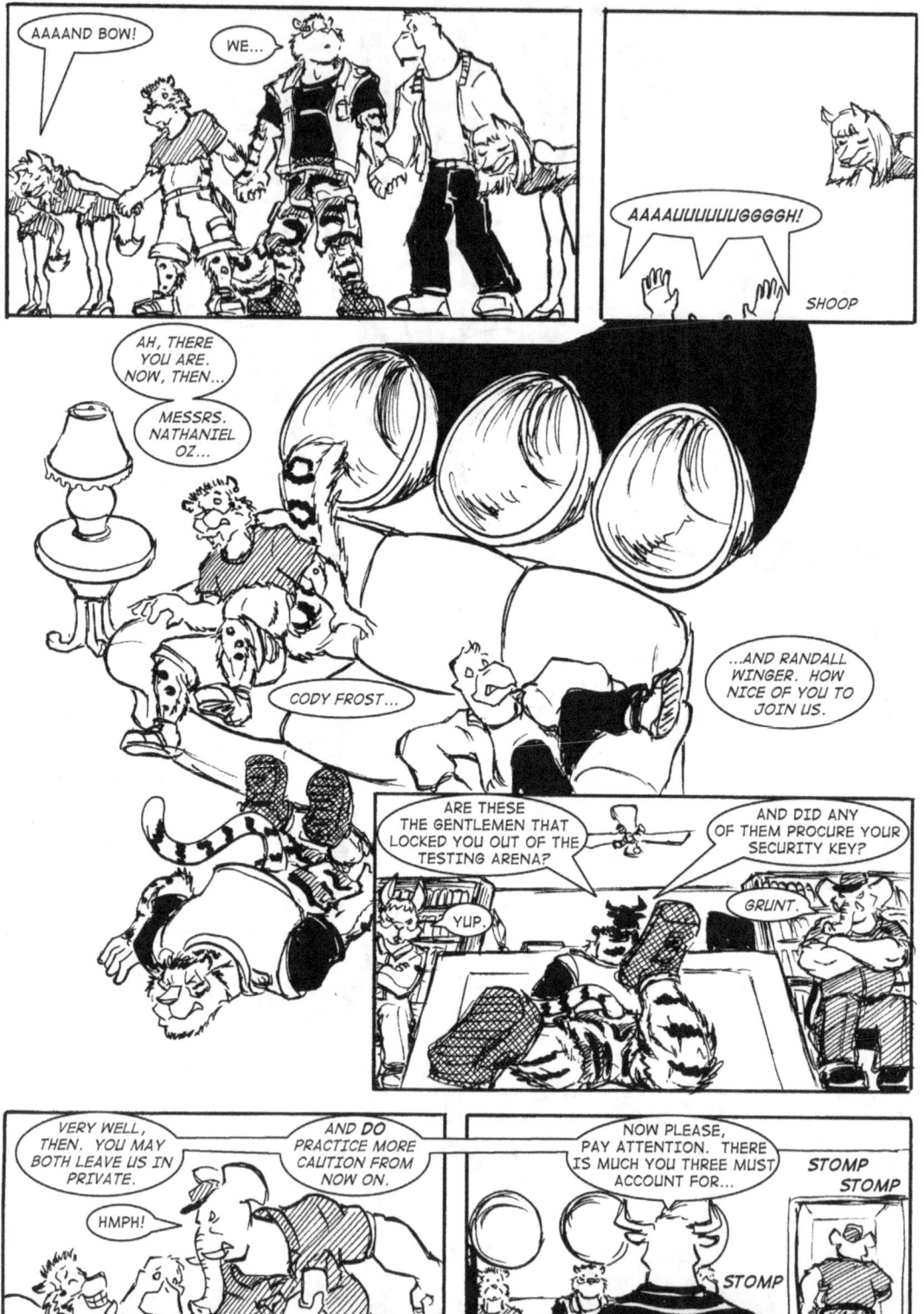

178

US?! YOU OUGHTA APOLOGIZE FOR USING US AS...AS BLOODY TEST SUBJECTS!

RANDALL, EASE OFF.

"TEST SUBJECTS?" HMM. AS I SEE IT, YOU THREE *TRESPASSERS* BLINDLY STUMBLED INTO THIS PREDICAMENT ON YOUR OWN ACCORD. YOUR TRANSGRESSION JUST SO HAPPENED TO BE DURING...

OUR ANNUAL TRADE SHOW.

YOU'RE KIDDING.

FORREST TECHNOLOGY EXPO

EDUCATING OUR FUTURE LEADERS IN SCIENCE DOES NOT COME CHEAP.

INVESTORS NEED TO BE CONVINCED OUR TECHNOLOGY IS CUTTING EDGE...

...AND BE ENTERTAINED IN THE PROCESS.

CLUB GLEEFUL DID THEIR PART, ALONG WITH THE FORREST DROIDS; IT'S NO COINCIDENCE THE HOCKEY GAME PRECEDED THE SHOW. THE PRESIDENT OF TOMIKARATA INDUSTRIES IS QUITE A FAN. HAPPILY, YOUR TEAM LOST.

THE GATEWAY GUN WAS PART OF THE EXPO?

ALONG WITH THE DREAM PROBE, THE BLOODLESS LASER AND HOLOGRAM CURTAIN. EVERYTHING YOU EXPERIENCED WERE ADVANCES THAT COULD BE APPLIED TO MEDICINE, SEARCH AND RESCUE, EXPLORATION...

SO GLAD TO BE OF SERVICE.

BEYOND ANYTHING YOUR JEJUNE IMAGINATION COULD EFFECTUATE... ESPECIALLY SINCE YOU THREE BARELY COMPREHEND THE MAGNITUDE OF YOUR INFRACTION. ONE LOST INVESTOR DUE TO YOUR DISTURBANCE COULD RESULT IN LAWSUITS THAT WOULD RUIN YOUR FAMILIES FOR GENERATIONS...

FORTUNATELY, THE SHOW WAS SOMEHOW A CONSIDERABLE SUCCESS.

TO SHOW MY APPRECIATION, I WILL MERELY SETTLE FOR YOUR EXPULSION.

WHAT?!

179

**LATE THAT SUMMER...**

CORNWALLIS TAKES THE FINAL STRAIGHTAWAY! THIS IS FOR THE RACE, THE TOURNEY, AAAND THE STEAK DINNER!

IT'S NOT OVER YET.

CORNWALLIS WINS! THE CROWD GOES WILD!

D'OH.

I KNOW YOU'RE GONNA DIG UP SOME CHEESY EXCUSE FOR LOSING. JUST GET IT OVER WITH ALREADY.

UMMM...I'M TIRED CUZ...JAMIE BROWN'S SET STARTED LATE?

MM-HM. THEN YOU WERE UP ALL NIGHT FANTASIZING ABOUT JAKE'S DANCING, RIGHT?

I DID NOTHING OF THE SORT.

YOU KNOW YOU'RE THE ONLY ONE I DREAM ABOUT.

FLATTERER.

184

188

189

C'MON, KRYS, WRAP IT UP.

HANG ON... SINCE I HAVE YOU HERE...GEORGE HAS A QUESTION FOR YOU.

MY MAN! HOWZIT GOIN?

JEFF SAYS HI.

GEORGE! 'SUP!

HEY GUYS... I WON'T KEEP YOU LONG.

BUT I'LL BE GETTIN' READY TO MAKE THE CUPCAKES TOMORROW, AND... WELL, SOMEHOW I CAN'T PICTURE YOU EATIN' SOME LITTLE POOF OF RED VELVET. YOU WANT ME TO MAKE YOU GUYS A BATCH OF SOMETHING ELSE?

OOH, LIKE...MINT CHOCOLATE CHIP, MAYBE?

YOU GOT IT!

THANKS, DUDE, YOU RULE.

NO PROBLEM. I MEAN, YOU EARNED IT... HOW THE HELL DID *YOU* GET ROPED INTO A BABY SHOWER? AT LEAST *I'M* GETTING PAID.

WHAT CAN I SAY, JEFF'S ONE EAGER UNCLE-TO-BE, AND SOMEONE'S GOTTA KEEP HIM OUTTA TROUBLE. ANYWAY, WE GOTTA JAM...

OKAY, HAVE FUN. YOU TAKE GOOD CARE OF MY LADY NOW.

ALWAYS! NOBODY'LL LAY A FINGER ON HER BUT ME!

AWW, WHAT ABOUT ME?

UH-HUH. DON'T MAKE ME COME DOWN THERE AND WHUP YO' ASS, JEFF!

THEN WE'LL FORCE *YOU* TO DANCE!

NEVER!! OKAY, GUYS, LATER!

ALRIGHT, THEN.

SHALL WE?

THE END

# Bonus Material

AS NOTED, I.S.O. ORIGINALLY STARTED OUT JUST A LOOSE ASSEMBLAGE OF THE VARIOUS BOYTOYS I'D CREATED POST-*CLASS MENAGERIE*. AFTER I DECIDED I ACTUALLY WANTED TO HAVE A GO AT MAKING A SERIOUS COMIC, SOME CHARACTERS NATURALLY COULDN'T BE FORCED INTO THE SETTING AS-IS, AND I DID A FEW REWRITES OVER TIME. HERE'S SOME CHARACTERS THAT WERE "LOST" DURING DEVELOPMENT.

### DUNCAN "DRAKE" BRAEBURN:

THE ORIGINAL GARDENER. HE WAS PURPOSELY DESIGNED TO BE A RIP-OFF OF GROUNDSKEEPER WILLIE FROM "THE SIMPSONS"—AN ILL-TEMPERED, LOUD, ATHLETIC SCOTSMAN—AND I MADE NO ATTEMPTS TO DISGUISE THAT. BUT I DIDN'T WANT HIM IN PRINT, AND IN RETROSPECT, THOR'S QUIETLY MENACING PERSONALITY WORKS BETTER IN THE STORY THAN DRAKE'S BLUSTER. I WILL NOTE THAT THE FIRE THAT FORCED THOR INTO HIS CURRENT JOB SITUATION WAS, OF COURSE, ORIGINALLY CONCEIVED AS STARTED BY DRAKE'S BREATH.

### MONTY SATTLER:

THE ORIGINAL SOUNDING BOARD FOR CODY. I KNEW FROM THE START HOW ANTI-SOCIAL CODY WAS GOING TO BE, AND THE ONLY WAY TO FACILIATE CONVERSATION ABOUT HIMSELF WOULD BE GIVING HIM A FRIEND WHO NEVER SPOKE. UNFORTUNATELY, I NEVER REALLY HAD A SOLID REASON FOR MONTY'S SILENCE WHEN HE WAS CREATED...I JUST THINK ENORMOUS BEEFY QUIET GUYS ARE FUNNY. SO HE WAS DUMPED IN FAVOR OF BORIS, WHO AT LEAST HAS THE EXCUSE OF HIS EATING HABITS FOR IMPEDING HIS SPEECH...PLUS WITH DRAKE GONE, ADDING ANOTHER REPTILE KEPT A BETTER SPECIES BALANCE.

### RUSTY ANGUS:

ANOTHER TORMENTOR OF CODY IN THE DORM, ALONGSIDE JAKE AND ZACH. AS AN IRON-LUNGED, HORNY, STUPID COW BOY WITH ASPIRATIONS OF A COUNTRY MUSIC CAREER (AND HE ISN'T HALF-BAD AT IT), HE WAS YET ANOTHER FACTOR DRIVING CODY OUT OF THE DORM AND INTO THE HANGOUT. THOUGH I LIKE ANNOYING CODY AND IT WAS NECESSARY TO HAVE HIM OUTNUMBERED AT FIRST, THERE WAS BARELY ANY REASON TO HAVE TWO CLUELESS GUYS IN THE COLLEGE, LET ALONE THREE. RUSTY SEEMED THE MOST OUT OF PLACE, SO HE WAS DROPPED AND NEVER REPLACED.

### REX CARRADINE/SILVIUS ARISTOTLE:

RECURRING HANGOUT CUSTOMERS, AND THE ONLY PRE-SET COUPLE. I WAS STILL IN THE MINDSET OF ANTI-LIMPWRISTED GAY STEREOTYPES, AND THESE TWO WERE ALL TIMED FOR A "GASP! YOU MEAN...YOU TWO ARE GAY TOO?!" MOMENT WITH CODY. BUT, WITH THE POINT ALREADY DRIVEN HOME AND THE CAST RATHER TOP-HEAVY, CUTTING THE DEMOLITIONS EXPERT AND FIREMAN-IN-TRAINING SEEMED TO BE A GOOD WAY TO AVOID VILLAGE PEOPLE COMPARISONS.

### THE HANGOUT STAFF, TAKE 1:

THE ORIGINAL STAFF CONCEPT; ALL FELINES, INCLUDING AN ADDITIONAL DEEJAY CHARACTER THAT WAS DROPPED WHEN I MADE THE HANGOUT MORE OF A COLLEGE SPORTS BAR THAN A CLUB. THE OWNER WAS STILL AN ACROBAT AND PRIZEWINNING BARTENDER BUT WAS A PANTHER, AND THE SECOND BARMAID WAS A SIAMESE KITTY. IT SEEMED TO MAKE MORE SENSE THEY HIRED CODY OUT OF NOWHERE, BUT IT ALMOST MADE THEM A LITTLE TOO CLOSE-KNIT. I PREFER A LITTLE DISTANCE IN CO-WORKER DATING.

HERE AT CLASSWORK COMICS, WE'RE WORKING ON I.S.O. MERCHANDISE FOR YOUR ENJOYMENT. UNFORTUNATELY, MOST OF IT SEEMS TO GET STUCK IN THE DEVELOPMENT PHASE. HERE'S SOME OF THE ABORTED ATTEMPTS AT PRODUCTS THUS FAR:

### JAKE PACKARD'S FASHION FOR MEN

REASON REJECTED: 0% BODYFAT MODELS ALL CAUGHT PNEUMONIA.

### GOAT-BOT

REASON REJECTED: ROBOT MODE DEEMED "NOT DEFORMED ENOUGH" IN LIGHT OF RELEASES OF *TRANSFORMERS THE MOVIE* AND *REVENGE OF THE FALLEN*.

### BECKY & SAM'S LINGERIE

REASON REJECTED: VINCE FAINTED AFTER A "WARDROBE MALFUNCTION" DURING THE MODELING SHOW.

### CHIBI-CODY PLUSH

REASON REJECTED:
FLUFF CAUSED DANGEROUS
STATIC BUILDUP.

### BORIS-BRAND
### FROZEN DESSERTS

REASON REJECTED:
VINCE GAINED FIVE
POUNDS JUST READING
THE INGREDIENTS.

### DOUG'S CONTRACEPTIVES
### FOR EXTRA-LARGE MEN

REASON REJECTED:
SOMEHOW THE TESTERS
JUST NEVER GOT AROUND
TO USING THEM.

### TODD VS THOR
### ACTION FIGURES

REASON REJECTED:
HOMOPHOBIC TAUNTS
IN VOICECHIP DEEMED
INAPPROPRIATE
FOR CHILDREN'S TOYS.

### "THE STALKER"
### SPYCAM

REASON REJECTED:
APPARENTLY VIOLATES
THE PATRIOT ACT.

### TY'S HANGOUT-BRAND
### BEER

REASON REJECTED:
UPSIDE-DOWN LABEL
CONFUSED CONSUMERS.

### BOBBLEHEAD ZACH

REASON REJECTED:
DESIGNERS UNABLE TO FIGURE
OUT WHY HEAD WAS ALWAYS TOO
LIGHT TO BOBBLE PROPERLY.

IT'S O.S.I. ("OF SEARCHING INWARDS"), THE NEW GLBT-FRIENDLY ROMANCE-COMEDY COMIC BY VANESSA SUZUKAWA. FOLLOW THE ADVENTURES OF CORIE FROST, A CLOSETED LESBIAN WHO FALLS FOR HER COWORKER DONNA. ASSISTED BY HER MENTOR JESS AND BEST FRIEND DOT, AS WELL AS NEW-FOUND ALLIES LORIS AND KATE, SHE STRUGGLES TO SIFT THROUGH HER REPRESSED IDENTITY SO SHE CAN SHOW DONNA HER TRUE INNER SELF. BUT THERE'S OBSTACLES ALONG THE WAY...DONNA'S OVERPROTECTIVE BROTHER SAMUEL; CLEO, THE IMPOSING GARDENER WITH A GRUDGE; CORIE'S NOSY, OVERLY HORMONAL ROOMMATE JANE; AND JANE'S DITZY FRIEND MACKENZIE. FORTUNATELY, THE HANGOUT, OWNED BY PRIZEWINNING BARTENDER DI WITH WAITER DECKER IN TOW, PROVIDES NEUTRAL TERRITORY FOR CORIE. WILL CORIE EVER FIND TRUE HAPPINESS? READ O.S.I. TO FIND OUT!

CORIE          DONNA          JANE          MACKENZIE

JESS          DOT          CLEO          SAMUEL

DI             DECKER            LORIS            KATE

EVERY ONCE IN AWHILE, I DEEM A PAGE UNSUITABLE, AND END UP REDRAWING IT...HERE'S A FEW REJECTS.

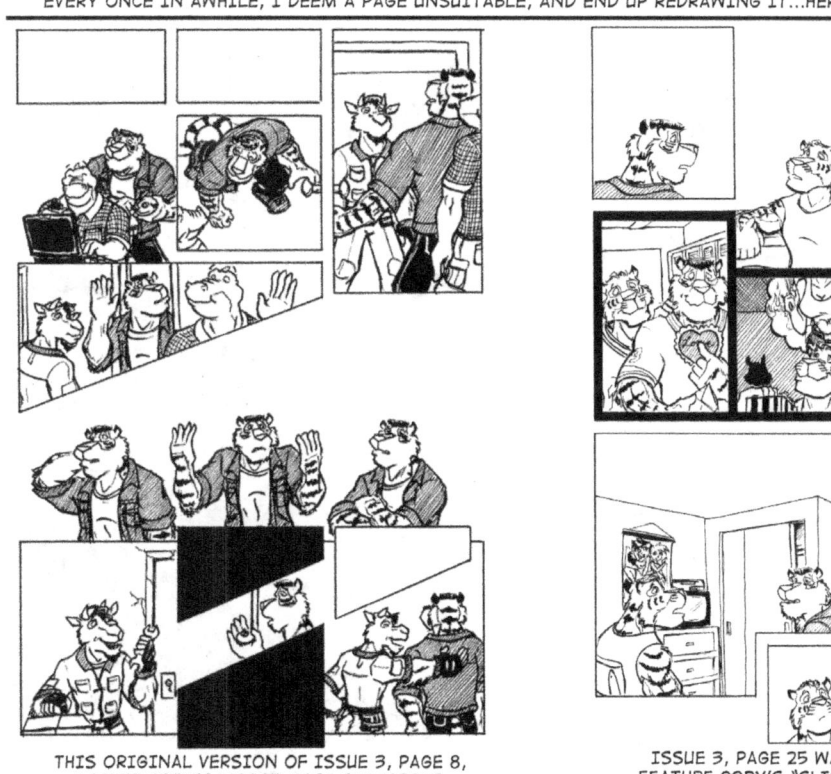

THIS ORIGINAL VERSION OF ISSUE 3, PAGE 8,
LACKED CODY'S WORST-CASE SCENARIOS
OF ASKING DOUG OUT.

ISSUE 3, PAGE 25 WAS LATER REDRAWN TO
FEATURE CODY'S "SLICE OF LIFE" FLASHBACKS
AS LITERAL SLICES OF BREAD

**199**

THESE ORIGINAL PAGES 10 & 11 OF ISSUE 5 WERE DRAWN WITH MINIMAL RESEARCH DONE ON WALL-CLIMBING. I MADE THE HARNESSES BACKWARDS, AND WHILE IT'S POSSIBLE TO HAVE AUTOMATIC BELAYING EQUIPMENT, IT'S NOT COMMON; IT MADE MORE SENSE FOR THEM TO BE CLIMBING IN PAIRS THAN SOLO. AFTER ACTUALLY GOING WALL-CLIMBING MYSELF SOMETIME LATER, I REDID THE SEQUENCE PROPERLY.

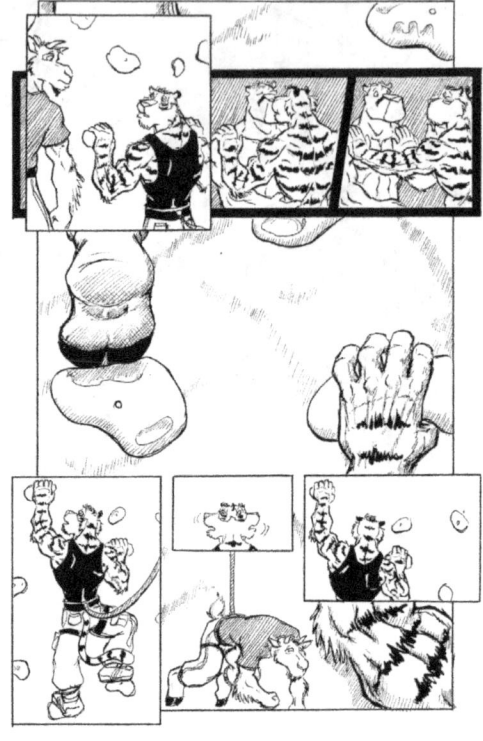

THIS WAS GOING TO BE THE COVER OF THE SECOND ISSUE, BEFORE I DECIDED I PREFERRED COVERS THAT

THIS ISN'T TECHNICALLY A REDRAW, BUT PAGE 32 OF ISSUE 7 HERE ENDED UP BEING REWORKED SO

AS RECENT ISSUES HAVE FOCUSED MORE ON MIXED-SPECIES COUPLES, I
THOUGHT IT WAS TIME TO EXPLAIN THE GENETICS IN THIS WORLD.

IF A COUPLE ARE COMPLETELY DIFFERENT
SPECIES, THE CHILDREN MUST MATCH THE
SPECIES OF THE PARENT OF THE SAME
GENDER. THUS, IF MAUREEN AND WENDELL HAD
CHILDREN, ALL SONS WOULD BE FERRETS,
AND ALL DAUGHTERS WOULD BE ALPACAS.
NO PHYSICAL TRAITS WOULD CROSS OVER.

IF A COUPLE ARE THE SAME SPECIES, ALL
TRAITS MAY POTENTIALLY MIX, REGARDLESS
OF GENDER. NOTE THAT CODY HAS HIS
FATHER'S FUR, BUILD, AND HAIR; BUT HE
HAS HIS MOTHER'S MARKINGS AND FACE SHAPE.
IF HE HAD A SISTER, SHE MIGHT RECEIVE A
SIMILAR RANDOMIZED MIX OF TRAITS.

FOR ALL OTHER MIXED COUPLES INBETWEEN,
THE MORE PHYSICAL RESEMBLANCE BETWEEN
SPECIES, THE MORE LIKELY THE TRAITS WILL
BLEND. HYBRIDIZATION MAY OCCUR WITHIN
VERY CLOSE RELATIONS (IE CANIDS, EQUINES),
BUT THIS IS RECESSIVE AND EASILY LOST
WITH SUCCESSIVE GENERATIONS. HERE, A
MALE DOG AND A FEMALE FOX PRODUCE
HYBRID CHILDREN OF BOTH GENDERS.

BEYOND A CERTAIN POINT, THE GENDER
RULES ARE THE SAME AS WITH DIFFERENT
SPECIES, BUT THERE IS STILL THE
POSSIBILITY OF MIXING SUPERFICIAL TRAITS
SUCH AS COLORATION, HEIGHT, BUILD, ETC.
HERE A BULL AND A MARE PRODUCE
CHILDREN WITH THEIR COLORATION SWAPPED.

HOPE THIS HELPS!

www.ingramcontent.com/pod-product-compliance
Lightning Source LLC
Chambersburg PA
CBHW080734250626
47170CB00010B/2821